Prolance

www.prolancewriting.com
California, USA
©2017 Minnah Arshad

ISBN: 978-0-9987527-5-4

Kindness is a Waiting Place

The life-changing encounter between
an American woman and a Syrian boy

MINNAH ARSHAD

PROLANCE

Dedication
To all the children in the world.
Dream and strive.

Chapter One

Shops and pedestrians crowd the streets. I smell pollution, pungent and overflowing in the air. But I also smell the roasted chestnuts, fresh fruit, and leather. I see young and old, men and women, all their faces muddled together to create one crowd. I think of home, and the cities I have visited there. All cities share the same way people blend into crowds.

Back home, most worries seem materialistic. Entire groups of people are labeled as scapegoats. Maybe it's here too. But there is that shock of reality that saves people from that same foul ignorance. How can people shut their eyes and ears to the world, to the truth, when it is shoved in their faces?

I remember the sight of a little foreign boy, curled to a dirty market wall, drenched in rain and blood, alone, young, and scared. This is real. This fear, this terror… it is the only reality that exists. Self-pity and empty worry disappears, replaced with war and stuttering hope. Scared of death, and terrified of life. Fear is pungent in the polluted air and controls souls that once had absolute certainty and innocence.

The cries of a child bring me back to the present. I turn, alarmed, but my worries are soon dismissed. I smile at the three children in the street, screeching and laughing with joy. I join them with a smile. What does it matter why? In an age like this, happiness is only accepted, not questioned.

But there is something else, too. These people have taught me that those who have seen nothing but death and brutality for years are the ones that have taught me happiness. A little girl who has never set foot in a school holds more wisdom than I will ever be able to.

Happiness can be created. But it can also be destroyed. The only question is, how do you choose?

A man behind a street stall calls out to me. He sells canned milk and tea bags. I politely decline, and walk my usual route, stopping by the same fruit stand as I have been for the past six days. Elias, I learned his name is, greets me with a smile. Little conversation ever occurs, but not from lack of trying. Neither person understands the other. Still, I feel I know the man.

He hands me the banana bread I point to, and I empty my change into his hand, sneaking in an extra coin. I walked away hurriedly, before he notices. He calls after me. I don't look back. We both know who needs the money more.

I only have one more day in Istanbul before it's time to go to the refugee camps in Syria. No more banana bread, shopping bazaars, or hilly roads. I'll miss this place. But I have plenty of adventures ahead. I have faith in how busy they'll keep me. Busy is good, though. Time is too precious to waste. There is so much we can do in this small world, yet people waste their days on nonsense. Giving back is a responsibility, and it is one that I am eager to fulfill.

A smile enters without my consent as I rip open the bagged bread. A sweet, fresh scent wafts into the air. I breathe it in, my smile deepening, before breaking into a chunk of it. The dense wheat is sweetened with pureed banana. Honey glazes the surface, and is unevenly distributed throughout the bread. There are walnut chunks too. But that is all. No spice, butter, sugar, or preservatives. It lasts two days, three in cold weather.

I have my fill of the bread, before breaking it into chunks and passing the rest to children like I've done the past six days. Most are happy to take it, but some barely notice I'm there. Still, I set a piece in their lap, knowing they'll eat eventually.

A scarf stand is up ahead. I try to bargain with a young man for six of them to pass to refugees. He's stubborn, however, or maybe I'm a bad bargainer. So I move on to the next. Once the scarves are bought and passed out, I buy bundles of toasted chestnuts. My Western taste is not acquired to them, but I find myself eating them every day. The rest are passed on to other refugees. Most are no older than fourteen, but none could I consider children. Still, I pass a few elders, and they take what I give with a smile. I arrive at the Grand Bazaar with sore feet, ripped running shoes, and burning legs. My honey colored hair is swept to the side, matted down with sweat. But I smile anyway.

The bazaar is a huge line of stalls underground. I walked down three flights of stairs, passing dried fruit stalls on the way. The first stand I stop at sells jewelry. Nothing catches my eye, so I move on, stopping eventually at a soap cart. They are all handmade, cut into rough blocks. A strong scent surrounds the murky stalls, and each soap bar is a different shade of a different color. A red bar catches my eye. It's the smallest block on the table, yet somehow it is the most eye catching. Suddenly, red is more than just something on a color wheel.

This shade in particular draws my eye. It holds volume, and calls for attention without desperation. It's overpriced, by double at least. The bar's edges are rough and cracked and a chalky substance coats all surfaces. He's a stubborn man, and lowers the price by only a couple lira. I buy it anyway.

I walk ten minutes before a marble collection stall catches my eye. There are charms carved out of multi-colored stone plates. I settle on a simple, elegant infinity charm. It's silver, with miniature stones lining the border. It has a royal blue cloth band that matches beautifully. I pay the money to the charming salesman, which he accepts with a sincere grin. I return the smile before continuing on as I tie the blue string to my right hand. The rest of my trip passes similarly. I walk until something catches my eye, mostly only to stare and take pictures. Few times do I leave a stall with a heavier bag and a lighter wallet. Still, every penny I spend seems worth it.

After two hours of strolling through the bazaar from end to end, I leave in search of food. My bag is heavy now, with a soap bar, a bag of dried cherries and roasted peanuts, a few souvenirs for back home, a large bag of my favorite tea blend, and three small earrings. The dried fruits and nuts I save for a snack, and look for street food. There is an Indian restaurant I tried once back home, but I ended the night with an empty gallon of milk and a burning mouth. But it had been worth it.

I buy a Turkish style wrap from the side of the road. The cooks call it a shawarma. It's filled with grilled chicken, vegetables, and a rich garlic paste. And although the lettuce is slightly wilted, and some of the tomatoes are bruised, it's one of my favorite things about this place.

After I finish the wrap by the fountain in front of the Blue Mosque, it is already 4:00. With an entire room left to pack, and a flight at 8:00 am tomorrow, little time is left. There is only one more place to go. And then I leave.

He hasn't moved.

Still curled up against the same market wall, dressed in nothing but filth, jeans, and a short sleeve shirt. Well, half of one. The banana I placed on his lap last night has been reduced to brown, delicate peels. At least he ate.

The little money left in my purse is spent on him. Most goes towards food and clothes. Powdered milk, a gallon of water, cheap biscuits, a wool sweater, and cheap shoes. And then I spend the remaining change on a small red apple. It's a luxury for the child, one I think he is more than worthy of deserving.

With a deep breath, I walk up to the boy and tap his shoulder. It's a gentle touch, gradual and wary. As expected, I get no response. It is only when I give him the clothes does he look up at me.

I stare, startled at his eyes. In another life, he would've been a lucky child. Handsome face, and what was once a burning light, now ashes. Now, I see nothing. No fear, no anger, and little sadness. He looks so empty. Perhaps he feels so too. But the thought only lasts a moment, before it is quickly dismissed. No. A blank mind is far too lucky for this child. While his eyes hold nothing, something tells me his heart tells a different story. In another world, the happier, more forgiving one, I may have noticed how beautiful the color of his eyes are. Green and gold, with long dark lashes. But now, all I see is a blank, slightly startled stare, and dirty skin surrounding his wide eyes. The beauty fades in my eyes, replaced with empty pain and painful emptiness. My heart breaks. My innocent, whole, relatively small heart chips. Maybe I give the piece to the unnamed child in front of me, or to a pitless well of doom. At least, from where I am looking.

"For you," my voice croaks. Maybe he understands, maybe he doesn't. This somehow seems insignificant. He nods either way, and slowly, cautiously takes the bag with wary, bony hands. He holds the bag on his lap, and grasps the handles tightly. It's the most emotion I've seen him show.

The sweater remains untouched. His lifeless stare is back, unnoticing of my presence. I sigh, grabbing the sweater and slip his skinny arms in. He looks at me once more. The shock has lessened, but there is still wariness. By the time I've zipped up the jacket, he is still staring. I smile before thinking. His gaze doesn't change.

I decide not to pester him about food. He'll eat eventually. But the blank stare… I want it gone. So I pat his head gently. He flinches. My smile drops, along with my hand.

Maybe my time is done here. I stand up, uncaring of the dirt that coats my jeans. Part of me hopes he'll stop me, and do something other than stare at a sad wall as he replays sadder memories. But he doesn't. By the time I reach the other side of the street, he's back to staring. I think about what I can do. Nothing comes to mind. So I walk to the bus station and go to the hotel. The ride home is spent in gloomy silence, as the city continues. And even after I have packed and gone to bed, the little boy stays in my mind.

The taxi driver honks as the car shakes over a bump in the road. I jump in my seat. The driver only smiles.

Chapter Two

My bag sits at my feet, neglected. "And you're sure there's no way I'm allowed in?"

The flight attendant nods blankly, still staring at her screen. "You must understand. There are certain safety precautions we must follow, as an organization. After this threat, we can't risk any more people by sending you in."

She stares at me, expecting a reply. But I have nothing to say.

"We could book you a flight back home."
I immediately refuse. "No. I'll wait until we get clearance to go."

The lady gives me that same blank stare. "But you may not get clearance for a long while. They take extra precautions with people from your organization."

She says it bitterly, as if it's my fault that the color of my skin determines the alleged value of my being. But I don't blame her. So when she asks to book me another hotel in the city, I tell her I'll take care of it. My attempted moment of kindness elicits no response. So I thank her quietly and walk away.

It is only once I reach the airport entrance that I realize I don't have anywhere to go. And no local currency. My initial nervous excitement for the prospect of working in a Syrian refugee camp fades into disappointment and uncertainty.

And then I remember what my mother used to teach me. Whenever you feel sorry for yourself, think about five people who have less than you. If your self-pity doesn't fade by then, you need medication. So I count. One, my mother; she was stolen from the right to live. Two, Bernie; the homeless man down the street. He is stolen from the right to shelter and food. Three, my group of children at the hospital back home. They have been stolen from the right to fair health. Four, the refugees of Aleppo. And five... my fifth is the little Syrian boy curled up against a dirty Turkish wall. The thievery committed against him cannot be expressed by words. I won't try.

The self-pity is long forgotten. And replaced with it now is a sense of hopelessness, and yet, somehow, emerging hope. How can I feel both at the same time? My train of thought confuses me, so I find a new track. First, I book a hotel. The rest will come.

Chapter Three

Since I liked the hotel the organization had booked me so much, and since I didn't know much about the hotels in the area (considering the unpredictable circumstances), I find myself in the same hotel as the one I'd just checked out of. The room is different, and it takes a certain amount of adjustment. My stomach aches for food, but I can't bring myself to go out into the city right now. So, with a twinge of guilt, and a flood of exhaustion, I call in a big ostentatious dinner platter. Kabobs, hummus, lentil soup... comfort food of the Arab world. The man on the phone cautiously reminds me that it's a two person platter. I can't bring myself to argue with him, so I ask for the billing total and hang up. With twenty minutes to spare before dinner arrives, I force myself up from the bed to shower. First, I open the suitcase I had unceremoniously packed, and dig through it until I find semi-clean pajamas, along with my Pantene two in one, and a luxurious bar of Dove, luxurious considering the cheap stuff hotels have.

The water runs cold, and the curtains are moldy, so my shower is quick, and I am out well before the food arrives, shivering but clean. The water here is somehow different from back home, and my hair still hasn't adjusted, so I spend another five minutes harshly brushing through tangled webs.

The food comes soon after the hair epidemic (which is readily forgotten), and I eat voraciously, while watching The Property Brothers show. I usually despise the show, but tonight, I don't mind it. The handyman twin is crabby, and the other twin looks like he's constantly facing some very intricate dilemma, but they're nice to look at and the before and after pictures of the houses are interesting.

But once my hunger dissolves, which is replaced with

food induced apnea, the show no longer is able to keep my attention. So I shut it off and lay down, right next to the half eaten party platter. And for some inexplicable reason, my heart aches. Maybe it's the unfortunate series of events of the day, or homesickness, or anxiety, or maybe even the overload on greasy kabobs that literally causes my chest to hurt. I feel such deep cutting pain, and I don't even know why.

It is in my lowest moments, moments like these, where thoughts of my mother drown me. She is embellished in my mind, and missed to an excruciatingly high degree. My vast memories of pain that are associated with her are forgotten, and all I remember is her wisdom, her love, her kindness. But mostly her presence. Knowing, even when we fought, I could always lean back on her.

A loneliness floods me like a storm. First, with soft, inclining waves. And gradually higher, higher, until land becomes sea. And nothing can stop its destruction. All anyone can do is wait for the storm to pass. Hope for it, until that too drowns.

So I let it come.

Chapter Four

My tears taste saltier than I remember since the last time I cried. And crying seems messier than I remember. Mucus runs like a waterfall from my nose, and my stinging eyes are bloodshot. The pillow is cold and wet, so I chuck it onto the floor and grab another.

Once the tears run dry, I expect some wave of relief. Or peace. Instead, all I get is a growing pit of loneliness and a red face. My head sinks farther into the pillow, and I stay still, just like that for so long, I almost believe I had left an imprint of my body in the mattress. The ridiculousness of my crazed thoughts scare me, so I kick off the covers and swing my legs over the side, sitting up. I feel goosebumps everywhere from the cold, but they don't fully register in my mind.

Nothing registers, except that I need to get out. Staying boxed in here is doing things to me. Crazy things, like watching Property Brothers and crying. So without thinking, since that never ends well, I stand up and tear off my pajamas, which land in a heap next to the disarrayed suitcase. I find stained jeans and a smelly t-shirt, which remains only half covered by my black coat. I put on shoes, get my purse, and get out of the confining matchbox.

The elevator is empty, and I feel the first blessing of tonight upon me. It feels strangely uplifting. I even smile at the man in the lobby. He grins back charmingly, as all the charismatic people do here. Even in my currently compromised state, I can appreciate that.

The bitter winds nip at my exposed hands. A shiver runs through my body, but the cold has become more bearable. Or maybe, it is me who has become more accepting of the inclement weather. Back home, people, including me, have enough time to complain about trivial things like weather, all while standing in big coats and sweaters. But here… here, there are fewer complaints about winter, while it is here that people suffer because of it.

This thought saddens me, so I rid my mind of it, storing it for a later time. For now, I enjoy Istanbul.

Chapter Five

By the time 8:20 arrives, the city has lifted my mood significantly. When all else fails (even kabob rolls), try merry company.

Still, one can never feel euphoric when walking in a place like this. With beauty, there is heartbreak. Children running around the streets, sometimes in bands, sometimes alone. Old men begging to clean your shoes so they can get just enough money to make it through another night. And finally, a middle aged man advertising for a restaurant.

"Welcome to the Blue Restaurant. We have all the Turkish signature dishes, including kabobs, fried fish, and shawarmas. Would you like to take a look at the menu?"

I halt in the middle of the street and look at him. The first thing I note is his English. He speaks flawlessly, with almost no accent. But he has the typical pale, Syrian skin, and his eyes are a pale blue. But there is something different about his stature. He carries himself as an educated man would. Straight posture, and a confident and steady gaze. His clothes are worn beyond repair, but they look ironed and washed.

Yes. He is certainly different from the rest.

I am still stuffed from my splurge in the hotel, but my tongue doesn't seem to notice. I hear myself saying yes, and moments later, right there on the street, I feel a greasy, laminated menu in my hands, and two warm brown eyes staring at me. This man has this knowing smile, as if he always knows what runs through my mind.

"Rotisserie chicken is our specialty."

I feel sick at the mention of food. My brain takes over. "I actually just ate dinner. And besides, I don't have any company to eat a whole chicken with. Thank you, though."

I slowly walk away, leaving my curiosity at the man's feet. But he persists. "What about dessert then? Or at least something to drink. We have mango lassis, and ganaffah. The Turkish are known for them." His smile is just as persistent. I have no time to say no, before he gestures me toward the restaurant with his hand and begins to walk, as if expecting me to follow. Something about his confident stature insists that I do.

So my feet begin to move, and I see a massive empty restaurant. Lights hang around the exterior, as if a party is awaiting you inside; the festive Turkish music does too. But the windows give them away. Inside is one beautiful, festive, empty hall. I see two groups dining, but no more. Well, I suppose I make the third.

"Your English is flawless," I hear myself say. But plenty more is implied.

"I used to teach at a university in Syria. I was well known as a professor; people all across the country came to sit in my classes. And then ISIS, or Assad, or perhaps the Western countries, bombed our city. What does it matter whose name is sprawled across the jet that drops it? A bomb is a bomb. And a death is a death."

My heart stills at his words. And his smile. He's smiling.

"I can't imagine going through that." They are the truest words I've spoken all day.

"I fled Syria and came here. My wife and kids… they're stuck back home. I try to send them money, but I don't make much. But I shouldn't complain. If it wasn't for Khalid, the owner of this restaurant, I would've been on the streets."
"You are on the streets," I say thoughtlessly. My face turns beet red, but the man only grins.

"But I get a paycheck for it. Most people aren't so lucky. But Allah bless Khalid. Whether I bring him two customers in a day, or ten. He always gives me the same salary."

A wave of humility washes over me. I have more than this man ever will, yet he has more goodness in his pinkie toe than I possess in my whole body. I can't help but see him as nothing short of a hero.

"So, what would you like to order? I recommend the mango lassi and ganaffah."

I laugh at his lightheartedness, and try to absorb his warmth. A blizzard is heading my way, and this man is a soft fire.

Chapter Six

The next morning, my slumber breaks at the sound of a ringing phone. The clock has only struck 8:00 and someone has dared to interrupt my peace. But curiosity gets the best of me, as it often has, and I answer groggily.

"Yes, I am Miriam Syed from Islamic Relief. I am calling about your delayed trip to Aleppo. You were on the… city cleanup group, correct?"

My mouth awakens faster than my brain. Something clicks. "Yes, yes. My flight… they canceled. Are we safe to go now?"

"I'm afraid not, ma'am. We apologize for the inconvenience. You have two options. The first would be to cancel your package to Aleppo, and we can book you a flight back home. We would pay only-"

"I'd rather stay in the city and wait. Is that possible?"

The woman's voice smiles. "Yes, that would be your other option. Unfortunately, we would not be able to cover your expenses in Istanbul. Also, we can't promise you'll be able to go to Syria, anyway. The flight to Aleppo and back home will still be covered, along with the package you had signed up for once you get to Aleppo."

"How long do you think it'll take?"

"Ma'am, I'm really not sure. It's incredibly-"

"Ball park it."

There is a pause in speech from both ends. I only hear Miriam's breathing and chaos through the phone.

"Probably one full week. They're saying we can go in a

couple days, but it will most certainly get worse."

A week. I feel myself getting wary. But then I think of what is waiting for me back home. Little comes to mind. So, in that very moment of lonely weakness, I dismiss her warning and book my hotel room for six more days.

But my heart doesn't panic or tell me to tread with caution, and this strengthens my resolve. I have been wrong on many occasions, more so than I have been right. But my gut? Not a single time.

Not until this moment. But I won't know this for another four days. And then the storm will come. Until then, I relish the calm.

Chapter Seven

My second night back in the hotel is spent eating to my heart's content (and to anxiety's fault), and scrolling through TV channels. I give up on Property Brothers, and I move on to bigger and better things, like Home Alone in Turkish and Everybody Loves Raymond. However, I've worn myself out of that too, and as I am scrolling through my last few channels I decide to shut off the TV. And then I see it.

The Turkish voice sounds frantic and mournful. But I barely hear it. All I notice is the image. Clear air turned to smoke, and not a single inch is left unscathed from it. Red and black flames consume a mass of concrete. There are men and women yelling frantically, sobbing.

And there are children, too.

Most lay idle on the ground. Flies touch their skin, and soot engulfs them. There is one child; his eyes are still open, mouth agape. And he's wearing a Messi jersey. He dies too innocent, too undeserving of death.

The screen goes blank. I see the remote in my hands before I feel it. And then the tears. Warm trails of salty liquid have reached my neck, down my shirt. I cry for the children who are dead. I cry for the children who must live after. And then I cry for everyone else, because none of them deserved such a cruel fate. I cry for myself, too. But mostly for the children.

Once the tears run dry, an absurd thought comes to mind. If I had to go through that, would I rather come out dead or alive? I don't coherently answer the question in my head. My answer scares me too much.

My eyes glaze over with tears again, and I let them do so, but only for a second. And then the moisture streaks across the palm of my hands, across my cheeks. The warmth of the sadness is gone. The assaulted tears are cold.

Now, I feel anger. It blooms in my heart, and I reach for my phone, going straight to the news app. What I see only makes the bloom in my chest enlarge. The Syrian bombing; a fleeting story. Maybe a headline for five minutes or so. But then somewhere else one man, one big popular man dies, and Aleppo's story is gone. Dissolved into absent air.

What child is deserving of such cruelty? How can we dismiss them so quickly? My heart thrums, palms sweating.

And suddenly, I feel urgent, impatient to absolve the world of this injustice. To make things fair. To do something. Something more than watch this on a hotel television and tremble about it.

I feel responsible. Isn't the bystander just as evil as the inflicter? And I don't like feeling responsible. My moral code, my security blanket, is ripped from me, and rightly so. It shouldn't have taken thirty two children's deaths to make me see this, but it did.

And now... now something must change. I must change something.

Chapter Eight

I expected my unbounded determination to fade with the night, but my heart staggers me. I wake at precisely seven o'clock, preceding my alarm by thirty minutes. I tie my hair up in a high ponytail, change into a fitted tie dye shirt, my army green jacket, thick khakis, and then lace up my sneakers, double knot. I mean business.

I stop by the ATM and withdraw more cash than I normally do. The air bites and snarls in cold gushes of wind, so I zip up my jacket, and pull on the hood. I feel the goosebumps before I see them. The tickles of hair wisping against frozen skin reminds me of the little boy, curled up against that damned brick wall. My heart aches so furiously, I am surprised by the sudden pain I feel, right in my chest. It is a feeling I am unaccustomed to. People know me as cold, stubborn, metallic. They would laugh if they saw me now.

The familiar sound of a man's laughter pulls me out of my spiral of grief. I look up, naturally, and my lips pull into a big smile without my consent. My feet move towards him, and I hear myself laughing warmly.

"Where you go?" the bread man asks.

I smile until my pearly white teeth show. "Nowhere at all." His eyebrows draw together in confusion, but his smile ceases to fade.

"One banana bread?"

I laugh, nodding. When I hand him the money, he shakes his head.

"You give me too much last time," the man says, his mouth setting firmly.

But my eyebrows pull together. "No, no." I push the cash and coins toward him, insisting he take it. Guilt begins to well in my chest, like an overwhelming wave washing over me. I extend my arm further.

I drop my hand for a moment. "Forget about bread money. This is about you. You need money."

"Yes. You pay for something, I get money. But no like this."

I stare at his unnerving blue eyes. He won't retreat; I can tell. So another plan forms in my head. He isn't the only determined one here.

"Fine. Give me ten bananas, and all the apples you have. And you have any more bread?"

He nods, but he looks wary of me. I can't blame him. "What you do with all this food? Party?" he laughs, charming as always.

That is one thing I have learned about these people. No matter how heavy the weight of the world upon them gets, they still throw jokes at you and grin widely. We do the same, but only out of politeness. A load of phony crap. But these people do it because they believe they were dealt the good hand, I think. No matter how awful life gets, it is always better than the next person. And if this isn't true at first, they go out and find a "next person."

My heart sinks and soars all at once for these people. For their courage, their heroism, their kindness, and their faith. And so, as I feel my inner turmoil grow into chaos, the words I tell the man calm me just the slightest.

"I give your fruit to the children." I feel myself smile, but only to placate him. But this disappears.

"You feed them?"

"As long as you accept the money."

He lists a price, and I give him ten more than he tells me. He accepts it wordlessly without counting, and hands me a bag. I walk away, this time with a purpose.

Chapter Nine

My back aches from the food's weight in my backpack, but no voice in my head moans about it. Being in Istanbul has made it difficult to complain about anything, really. All my problems feel like a blip in the sky, while here, people deal with nothing but black holes.

Today looks beautiful. Grey cobblestoned streets, pedestrians, taxis, buses, and cars line the roads. The sun is near its highest point, blindingly bright, and not a cloud shades me from it. I squint in the light that bathes me and the city's every crevice. That brilliant star is the most beautiful. But right next to it are the little shops I see on both sides. Such a spectacular sight is unfit for today's miseries. It feels contradictory. I see one thing and feel another.

Even in my winded state, I can't help but appreciate this, right here. A certain acceptance befalls me, and I myself think in the midst of the crowd. This is life. I see the faces of Syrian children, the footage on the news, Arab headlines and all. But I also see the face of a Syrian professor, who fled his country and family to come here and be a restaurant advertisement. The Arabs' classier version of a man on the street wearing a hotdog suit. But the pay is no more dignified.

All his wisdom, these childrens' innocences… it would be an injustice to society to steal them from us. I want so badly to help, but what can I do? I'm just a rich, privileged white woman. Even then, I come here to help anyway, and what happens? That too gets canceled.

I must help at least the children. And if I can't go to Syria, I'll do it here. I stop walking and open my backpack, pulling out the grocery bag of food. I'll start with this.

I don't walk far before I see three children jogging

down the streets. The same three children I had seen much earlier. A teenage girl in hijab, a long sleeve anime hoodie, and ill fitting jeans. A boy, maybe twelve, in a Ninja Turtles shirt that falls to his knees and baggy khakis that tug on his cracked muddy sneakers. The last is another girl, not a day over eight. Her braided hair reaches her waist, but it looks frizzy and unkempt in the front. She's wearing a Minnie Mouse shirt that barely reaches her hips, a dirty white long sleeve shirt underneath and grey sweatpants.

I hurry my walk, afraid to lose sight of them. I pull out the loaf of banana bread and run to the oldest girl. She looks at me warily, but the two young ones continue to run around eccentrically. She calls out to them in Arabic, and they come back to her, still giggling. I continue to stare at her, until I realize that this is the part where I should start smiling. I had this entire conversation planned out. But no words come out of my mouth, and I stand there, stiff as a plank. I pull out the bagged bread in a hurry, or at least I try to. The bag tips and all the fruit falls out. I am left holding the bread by my fingertips. I am about to pull it all back, but one look up and I'm lost. The other two stop giggling, and stare at the ground with a wild, hungry gaze. I expect them to run to me and take it, but instead, they stare at me and motion to the fruit with their hands. They begin talking in Arabic, and it sounds like a desperate plea. So I see my hands put the fruit and bread back in the bag, and feel the cobblestone beneath my hands. I feel my lips pull upward, and lastly, I feel my arm move forward and hand the children the bag. All of it. Gone.

The oldest girl clasps her hands on my shoulders and she whispers in Arabic. And then she's gone chasing after the children. I stand there motionlessly, and watch as they run to the sidewalk and stand around the bag, heads crowded in. A shopkeeper yells at them, and they attend to him only partially, moving further from him. And then it's as if the world disappears around them. The boy's hand delves into the bag first, but the oldest girl slaps his hand. She pulls out the apples first, handing one to each person, ending with herself. They eat it like savages, and when they're done, not even the seeds remain.

Next is the bananas; one for each person. They eat slower this time, but it seems controlled, like they want to make it last longer. And then the bread; each person gets a chunk of it. The girl stares at it, mouth gaping. The younger two eat with their palms, shoving fistfuls of food into their mouths.

And then the most beautiful thing happens. The oldest is stowing away the food, even as the youngest two beg for more. But then the chatting stops, and all three children spot an old woman rocking on the floor on the sidewalk. She wears a black full length dress and matching hijab. They call it an "abaya." The kids walk up to her, pull out a banana, peel it open, and place her hands on top of it.

And then another. Two sisters are standing, hunched on the side of the road. The three children walk up to them, and hand each sister an apple. The girl's grasp on to the oldest child's shoulders, thanking them in Arabic. And in that moment, I desperately wish I knew the language of the land, just so I could fully understand the beautiful acts unfolding in front of me.

The sound of two men shouting distracts me from the scene. I turn to my left, and there they are. One snatches a pair of shoes from the other. It escalates to tackling, and two men are forced to interfere.

The sight disheartens me. But it is a reminder that there are bad people everywhere. But with the burden they carry that people elsewhere are free of… it makes me wonder if it is an equal scale.

Chapter Ten

The sunlight is beginning to fade, and I wonder if I should go back. But the empty hotel room feels so lonely, and well… empty. I decide against it, and search for a place to eat. In my entire trip, I've never been to a restaurant twice. It feels wrong, when there is so much more to discover. But tonight, I am in search of something familiar. Safe. Known. So I rack my brain for a place I have been to, searching through my long, long inventory.

Finally, I settle on the one I discovered on my walk after my little breakdown, the one with the Syrian professor. My wallet has lightened significantly since this morning, mainly due to all the food and scarves I bought. So I force myself to walk to save myself the expensive fare of a cab. My sore feet burn, but the worst is the cold. The temperature has fallen drastically after the sun separated, and I feel my neck growing sore and scratchy. I think of my mother, scorning me for not wearing my scarf. She would grab me by the shoulders, and wrap it around herself, in this ridiculous fashion. I would whine about how funny I looked, and she would tsk at me, and then sigh as if I was the biggest burden on the planet. But we got along okay. I just wished I appreciated her more, instead of hoping, wishing she was more like me. Now, I kind of miss it. I just miss my mother.

The only thing I don't miss about my past is me. God, I hate the person I was. Most people see the glass as either half full, or half empty. I would probably tip the water out, then complain about how the cup was completely empty. Even when I had so much to live for, I only saw the bad. I hate that. I think if I hadn't been so busy wishing all the time, I could have spent much more time appreciating my life for what it was, for what I had.

My thoughts run dry, at least for now. So I look around me, soaking it in. I smell the roasted chestnuts and fruit on display. I see the crowd of pedestrians and picture perfect street shops. But I also smell the burning of rubber on the pavement, the smoking fumes from cigarettes. I see the lonesome children, running on streets, and curled up against them. I see the beggars, young and old, and I see all the people that pass them by. It serves as a firm reminder that life is both beautiful and ugly, and those who think otherwise are either fools or very desperate to believe a lie. Probably both.

Chapter Eleven

Much to my chagrin, I don't spot the mystery man at his regular post outside the restaurant. I think about turning around and finding somewhere else to go, when I realize how ridiculous I'm being. And what does it matter if he isn't here? I came for the food, didn't I? So with this insight, I continue my walk down to the restaurant. I walk in, yet again overwhelmed by the royal gold tapestries and heavy music. The light is soft and overwhelming, all at once. And in the midst of this strange elegance, there is a fish tank. Its form is plain glass and black rim. The glass is dirty with fingerprints and smudges, but the interior is perfect. Clear, tranquil water, and healthy orange fish swimming around. There are these gold decorative pieces that sit inside the tank on top of the fake rocks. I find it both endearing and hysterical. I've certainly never seen that before. But somehow, it works.

I sit at a table for four, since the restaurant is almost vacant, save for multiple servers and two families dining. This part feels wrong. I feel like there should be more people, more sound, more laughter. Instead, there is a relative silence. I say relative, only to acknowledge the whistles of the wind, the clattering of the silverware, the occasional whispers. But mostly, there is silence.

A server rushes to my table and, with unbelievable cheer, hands me the menu. I thank him with a smile. His strange glee is not off putting; he exudes cheer. I look at the dirtied menu, feeling the grease stains rub onto my hands, and smelling the oil like it has been burned into a candle. But I find this okay, and focus on the items.

Everything is written in Turkish, so I look around for pictures but come up empty handed. I'm just about to pull out my mini Arabic to English dictionary, when I hear a voice call out.

"Miss! I didn't think I would see you again," I turn around and greet the booming, warm voice. The professor. I immediately smile. "Well, I figured I would give the food here a try, since all I'd eaten last time was the milkshake." He laughs at this. I join him, but only to not look a fool. It doesn't appear to work.

"I didn't know I was so funny."

He laughs again, at my expense. "Not milkshake, Miss. It was a lassi. Mango lassi."

He talks slow, as if I am an infant. And perhaps I am, in the foreign language department. But the man continues to smile, so I find it difficult to feel insulted.

"So what do you suggest I get?" I ask.

His eyebrows draw together. "Uhh, do you like beef?" I nod.

"How about beef kabobs with Turkish rice, hummus, and a small salad?"

I laugh. "That sounds like a lot for a party of one."

He laughs. "One person platter. You will like it."

"If you say so. I'm trusting you," I say seriously, but my smile betrays me.

Then he is gone, and I am left to the relative silence. When there is little that goes into my ears, my mind generates noise. I feel myself think a hundred thoughts at once. The professor, a catchy song lyric, the cold weather, my life back home… Crowded parties have less sound than my mind. I wish it was different. I feel like everything rushes by. So much all at once, and even after almost thirty years of experience, I still feel like life is one big game of catch up. Always two steps behind.

But there are steps I have moved forward. They are fewer, and usually less upscale, but they exist. And they are a big part of who I am today. I think signing up for that Syrian Aid trip, and then flying out here to Istanbul… those are one of my steps forward. And I also think, that no matter what happens, if I go to Syria, or if I don't, this trip will not be forgotten.

A waiter comes back with my "one person platter", which could easily feed three. Five if they had small appetites. The waiter laughs at my gaped expression, but his blue green eyes are twinkling and his stubbled face pulls into a smile. I use hand motions and small words to ask where the professor is. The man tells me he is working. I guess that means he is outside, advertising. So I forget about him and look at my meal, inhaling, salivating, and then filling my plate to eat. The rice is buttery and filled with toasted nuts and miniature strands of something akin to pasta, only better. The meat is tender and filled with flavor. Strangely, Turkish food is not spicy as I expected. Everything here is intense and flavorful, but it doesn't have that burning spice other cuisines do. For that, I am grateful.

I eat until I am satisfied. I still have platefuls of food

on the table. Guilt churns inside me at the thought of throwing it away. So I ask for boxes to put the food in. They laugh. When I don't laugh with them, they tell me they have plastic bags. No boxes. So I ask for Styrofoam bowls and plastic forks. They look at me like I'm crazy, but moments later, they are back with exactly what I had asked for. I take what they give, grab the ladle, and get to work. A spoonful of rice, a few strips of beef, some hummus, pita, and fattoush. I put one falafel in each bowl.

I am on my third bowl when I see the professor return. His face is red from the cold, especially his nose, like Rudolph. His breath is heavy but his posture remains straight, strong. He walks over to me, and stops next to the chair on my left. No words, just a strong, steady gaze. I decide to break the ice.

"Hi," I say, smiling.

He bows his head in greeting. "What are you doing?" I laugh. "Well, what you got me certainly wasn't for one person. I'm not sure how much you think I eat. But, anyhow, there was a lot of food leftover, so I figured I would pack the leftovers and hand them out."

His neck pushes back, and his smile disappears. "To who?"

"To the people on the streets."

He stays standing, but only for a moment. And then he is gone, still void of a smile. My frown deepens, and I wonder what I said to upset him. But then he is back, this time holding a box of aluminum foil. The box is covered in Turkish and a strange picture of a live chicken, but I accept it with a wide smile.

"The food would get cold, open like that in this weather," he says. The smile is back, but this time, it is different.

Softer, emotional.

"It is very kind of you to do this. I see people throw away food every day. And then they walk out of the restaurant, and children run up to them, begging for something, anything." He is angry now, and disappointed. I can't blame him. I think of what to do to keep his mind away from the dark place it is headed for. So I offer him the food. "You could just get a new plate and take some food if you like."

At this, he laughs. "I work at a restaurant, with a kind man as my boss. He lets me eat from his kitchen. Alhamdulillah. I am grateful. I have known true hunger, if only for a short time. And... and I am glad to be rid of it."

Pity settles in my heart first. And then embarrassment takes over. "Of course. Sorry, I didn't mean to assume--"

"No need to apologize. I would've thought the same about a poorly dressed man on the streets, like myself."

He laughs at his own strange humor and I feel weird to join him, so I smile and nod. I am unaware of who I am placating. Him? This man doesn't care about social niceties. He doesn't have time to. For me, then. I don't know. The placate process is ingrained into me. I used to think it was an annoyance, an unnecessary blockade between people. But now, I see it as a luxury. I am glad I have the time, the energy, and the money to worry about such trivial things. I am glad I can worry about socially acceptable ques.

And, dear God, I am ecstatic to not be him, this poor man in front of me. It's an awful thought, and I am disgusted with myself for thinking it, but it couldn't be more true.

I am unsure of what he sees in my eyes, but I don't believe he approves of it. So he looks down, closes his eyes, and the next time he is looking at me, those irises are guarded, and his smile is big and jolly. I suppose the art of placation exists to some extent in every place of the world.

"Great to see you again, Miss. Please come again. Good for business," he laughs.

Yes. I suppose it does.

Chapter Twelve

I have become obsessed with checking my phone. I wait for the call to come, the call telling me that I am set to go to Syria, that the bombing is clear, that it is safe. But the strange insistence to repeatedly check is driving me mad, so I push the cheap, slide open phone into the depths of my back pocket, and settle my hands in the front two.

I decide to make it today's mission to appreciate the city. While I understand my own apprehension to do what I came for, everything happens for a reason. And this city is so beautiful and full of life; it would be disrespectful and unappreciative not to soak it in.

There is one sight I am yet to revisit as of my Istanbul trip 2.0. That little boy near that restaurant I went to for what was supposed to be my last dinner. "Shish Kabob" I believe it was called, so I get into a taxi and tell the man the restaurant. Then I pay the fare, and climb out.

Traffic is heavier than usual, maybe because of the timing. I am not so accustomed to this city to know the rush hours. Still, "Shish Kabob" has room for one more, at least, so I go in and sit at a table. Considering my cheap choices I make for restaurants, I have become rather accustomed to the grease on the menus, and the torn leather chairs. American restaurants aren't always clean either, they're just better at hiding it.

I see the waiter that served me last time, but I don't expect him to remember me. But he does, and is soon walking right over to my table.

"You come back, huh? Enjoy the food?" he speaks in broken English. Yet he says so much in so little. I almost envy it.

"Yes, the food was perfect. What do you suggest I get this time?"

He looks at me confused. I point at the menu, and repeat, "To eat? What should I get?"

"Ahh, yes! Chicken kabob too good. You like."

I get monumentally less food than the last time, so I end with no leftovers. Forty minutes later, I am back on the streets, with a full stomach this time. And then it happens. My heart senses him before my eyes do, like a magnet to metal. And then I'm walking toward the boy. Because that is what this boy will do. He's already taken so much of my heart, and he hasn't spoken a word to me. He's never even looked at me.

He's still wearing the jacket I gave him, and the scarf too. The banana peel is gone, but I see the tip of a plastic bag on his left. Maybe it's wrong that my heart warms at this, but it does. He's clutching that bag like a lifeline, and he's there. Right in front of me, against that same alley wall. The first thought that comes to me is absurd. Don't his knees ache, bent like that? And his back looks permanently curved, like an old man with scoliosis. I feel my knees bend until my American Eagle jeans touch the ground. I flinch. The cobblestone is wetter and colder than I expected. The chills run through my legs first. And then the wetness is through my jeans and on my skin. And it hurts. The floor is rough and sharp and I almost stand up because my knees feel like they're on fire.

But I force myself still. Maybe out of guilt, because this boy, he isn't immune. He still feels the same coldness and wetness and roughness. Maybe I just stay like that so I can understand him, even if just for a moment. Who would do this to themselves?

People bypass us, stare at me, ignore the boy. I feel the wind of people's footsteps. I hear the pit-pat of the shoes, the indistinguishable chatter, the soft wind of the city. I smell the roasted chestnuts, the heated scent of people crammed like this, and that distinct smell of city and pollution. And yet... yet that all fades into background, and the cameras zoom into just this. Me and him. Him and me.

He looks at the brick and mortar, a million miles away. I keep my hands at my sides, and stay where I am. Something tells me that this boy likes his distance. So I give it to him.

But then he does something that has me taken aback. He looks up. He looks up and he stares right at me. Big green orbs with flecks of dull gold, maybe bronze, dirt marring the sides of his face. He has these long, gorgeous eyelashes, a small nose, and a perfect mouth. His hair falls to his eyebrows. It is a medium brown, and I see the grease and blood and dirt, even under the dim moonlight and shadowed city lights.

He studies me. I suddenly feel self-conscious, wondering what he sees. And what he doesn't. My heart beats faster, and my usually ice cold hands get clammy with sweat. And this kid is just staring at me.

What am I supposed to do? Do I say something? What was I thinking coming here?

This boy probably wants to run away. I tell my aching feet to scoot back so he can run if he wants to, but they stay frozen. And then someone carelessly kicks my back and I am shoved forward. And then I move back, just as much from instinct. I am closer to the wall, and for a moment, I forget his eyes are still on me. But then I look up at him, and the moment is gone. We stay just like that for a while, looking at each other, unsure of what to say. Or maybe that's just me. I don't think this kid talks. Or if he can, he chooses not to.

His eyes stay on me, but his back leans against the wall, as if relaxing, even just a little. It warms my heart, and I feel a stupid smile on me. But then he turns to the wall, and his arms stiffly reach for the bag. He gets it, and then, like a robot, hands it to me. I shake my head furiously. "Oh no. I don't want the bag. For you."

He looks at me unsure, so I take the bag and set it back where it was. He looks up at me, surprised this time. And then he sighs and closes his eyes. I think he might be sleeping, but his arms move around him, hugging himself. I see my hands take the extra scarf from the bag and hand it to him. His eyes open, but his hands stay still. So I drape the thick brown scarf over his shoulders and reach into the bag, pulling out an orange, peel it for him, break it into pieces, and then I take his cold dry hands, and place the fruit inside them. He stares at me, mouth open, and then looks down to his open hands, and then back to me. He stays like that, mouth still agape. And then there is this beautiful shift from cold nothingness to blurred skepticism. This is a step forward, and that is all I ask for.

And that is how we sit together on the side of the painful, cobblestoned streets, staring at the city. And while the small shards of stone continue to dig into my backside, that too, fades into the background. And then it is just us. Me and him. Him and me.

Chapter Thirteen

I get to my hotel room at midnight, and a voice in my head berates me for staying out that late, alone. But I swing that voice with a baseball bat, and my smile persists. And then I climb into the shower and wash the grime from the day, and the aches from the night. My legs, feet, even my chest hurts.

And somehow, the pain reminds me of a certain green eyed child. And I can't help but think what Advil he has for his aches. What shower does he have? And how safe does he feel out there on the streets, all night and all day, completely alone? And then I'm thinking about all the children of Syria, without a family or a home. All those children, all that pain. That one boy is exactly that. One boy. His suffering is awful enough, but a country full of children like that? My heart aches, and the shower, the medicine... nothing gets rid of this ache.

My face is wet, and it isn't from the hot jets of water from the shower.

No. It is from the pure agony I was yet to discover until I came to Istanbul, the city of sights. And I saw things I never wanted to see. Never dreamed of seeing. Little boys and little girls, curled against cold streets. A teenager watching over four children running through the streets. A former professor, who, once upon a time, received standing ovations for his lectures. And now he advertises for a failing restaurant on the streets.

All this pain. All this suffering. And the saddest part is that it doesn't have to be that way. If the rest of the world came together, and genuinely tried to fix this, they could. And yet, instead of compassion, these children get wealthy countries unwilling to help. Instead of open arms into the land of freedom and opportunity, these people, babies, mothers, grandmothers... they are banished from my country. And, consequently, banished from hope. Or at least the prospect of it.

My mother always told me how unfair the world was.

And I would nod along and agree, but only to please her. Because the thing was, life did seem fair. I went to a nice school, I got to be the class's desk inspector, and when our parents were home, we had game nights on Friday. I lost monopoly every time, but all was well since I won Scrabble every time. Even Cindy the Sissy didn't tip my world over the edge. Life was good. It was fair.

But then mom died, and my world didn't only tilt; it flipped over and imploded into a million pieces. Like a brand new Range Rover going into flames, out of nowhere. Sailing smoothly, then combusting.

Then life cooled down. The fire truck came and things got better. I pushed myself to therapy, I swallowed my pride and then my pills. And then slowly but surely, I got back on my feet. The car was rolling. Cautiously, painfully, but rolling. And then I came here. And it was like a covered wound got ripped open. And I'm lost and lonely, like a little girl washed up on an isolated island. And I have these wild animals, these night terrors chasing after me.

I stand under the shower until my fingers look pruned, my hair is dry, and I am dehydrated from the intense heat of the water. I walk out to the room and drip across the tiles and carpet. My footsteps are slow and uneven. I feel my body turn to ice in the frigid hotel room, goosebumps across my skin, and tremors down my spine. And then I am dressed in stained pajamas, and tucking myself in, under the comforters. And even as my body resembles a slow moving robot, my mind races, a hundred miles a minute.

The rumors about hotel sheets. The Istanbul bathrooms. And yes, yes of course, the little boy curled against the street. But I also think about my family back home. My mind does a speedy time difference conversion, and I learn that it is about six in the morning back home. I see my dad, asleep, or at least in bed. He never wakes up before ten now. My sister is out for a run, and then she'll come home at precisely eight. She will shower and then she will get ready for breakfast with her friends at IHOP. Meredith has mild OCD, so no one ever gets to give her crap about such strange routinely behaviors. Mom would reprimand anyone who so much as breathed in Mere's direction the wrong way. God knows she would never do the same for me. But as one year ended and the next began, I came to accept this, or at least push it to the back of my mind. And slowly, Mom's obvious greater love for my crazy sister hurt a little less, and breathing around both of them became a little easier.

But I don't believe I ever became okay with it. I justified it, I ignored it, I hated it. But never once did I feel at peace with it. And now, all of a sudden, my own worth feels minute compared to the greatness of this pain people experience here. And now, even my safety net of self-pity has been ripped from me, and I am falling. Falling, falling, and so desperate to land, yet even more terrified to see what happens if I do.

There is one rope I have been able to hold on to. And that is the rope of charity. Helping others helps me. And that is why I came here, on this trip to Syria. And yet here I lie, in a hotel room, trembling freezing in a beautiful city. My mind is a whirlwind of inky black. I took one step forward and life dragged me ten steps back. The world is cruel, cruel, cruel. I think about the professor in the restaurant. He had experienced so much suffering and loss, and yet he smiled as if he was the luckiest man to ever live. He laughed like kindness was infinite. He displayed kindness like people were ever-deserving of it. And he was at peace, as one looks on a gorgeous island resort. Not in the middle of a civil war. He blew my mind away.

And then I think about the band of four children, three boys running in glee down the streets, and one half-heartened girl dragging her feet to keep up with them. They were happiness in a Kodak framed picture. At least the boys were. That girl looked resigned. And yet, even as her feet dragged, they moved forward.

And then I feel for that boy. He was a sad story left untold. I don't think he even cared about living anymore. I don't think he cared about caring to live anymore. I try to imagine having so much darkness in my life, so little light, that I don't even care to live it anymore. I don't even care to end it. I try and I fail.

Chapter Fourteen

Robert Ingersoll once said, "We rise by lifting others." My fourth grade science teacher had a big poster of this quote in her room, and I sat right across from it. I remember the first few days in her class, I feel like the poster was up close, right in my face. Eventually, it blended into the background, like things often do. I grew used to its presence, and so I stopped noticing it. The poster is still imprinted in my brain, like a bright inky stamp.

It is strange that things you long remembered appear when you most need them to. I think this thought, and I feel surprised. It is the first positive thought I have had in days. And it is rather timely.

I fall asleep at a ghastly time, and wake up too soon after, around five. My head hurts, and I blame it on my current insomniac state. I use the hotel's coffee with reluctance. My mother's voice reprimands me, telling me that caffeine is not a replacement for sleep. But I ignore it.

My stomach burns from the acidic drink on my long empty stomach, but I remember my motivation, and I ignore this too. And then I search (rather barbarically) for the hotel legal pad and pen, and sit at the brown desk. This is my written works:

List:

-bread (from store near MJ's)

-fruit: oranges + apples + bananas

-new shoes

-pack of socks

-jacket

-toy?

The last one feels both silly and giddy. That boy barely eats, so I highly doubt he's interested in some toy. But the minuscule possibility of a small spark of joy, no matter how improbable, is enough to turn the small giddiness into a bounty of excitement. My brain goes into a frenzied overload. I think about all the possibilities, and for those few moments, my world becomes a wonderland, and I forgot about limitations.　　　The barbed wire is gone; the cattle roams free.

But then my stomach growls, and I am grounded back to reality. And maybe that isn't such a bad thing. The world I live in doesn't feel so harsh today. The sunlight is softened by clouds through the windows, and while the air is dry and stale, I feel a warmth blanket over me. The barbed wire is back, and the cattle stays restrained. But they are still roaming.

Chapter Fifteen

I wear my favorite army green jacket today, the one that almost touches my knees. My black pants are clean and crisp, and my shirt is the color of a starlit night sky, and soft like clouds. My hair is neatly combed and tied into a ponytail. My shoes are still the same worn brown boots, but I wear them for comfort, since I expect an abundance of walking today. Or at least I hope for it. I add my maroon beanie- the one my sister knitted for my birthday-, and then I am out with an unsafe amount of cash and a fully charged phone. And of course, the list.

The breakfast buffet is open, so I opt out of street food and trade it for a free meal with heating inside. There is a cereal bar, eggs in a million different forms, Turkish pancakes, colorful bite sized fruit, and a long line of buffet food. I get Cheerios with whole milk, a custom made omelet with a variety of vegetables, and one pancake. My plate looks bare, but after the horrors of poverty I have seen in the past days, I have an aversion to wasting food. I eat alone, and I eat quickly. The coffee tastes better here, so I have another cup of it with my pancake.

As I eat my cereal, I look around. It is amazingly absurd, to see people of all ethnicities in one hotel. There are Americans, British, Germans, Mexicans, Arabs, and Africans. A Muslim lady in an abaya smiles at me, and I am once again floundered at the kindness and normalcy of these people. I don't meet a lot of foreign people where I live. Muslims are displayed as either violent enemies or waif-like, ignorant creatures who blindly follow a mellowed, manipulated version of radical true Islam. And to be frank, I mostly believed in the second theory. I pitied them for their ignorance, for their blind faith, for the oppression of women. And yet I am embarrassed and greatly humbled by my realization at my total distortion of truth. These people are neither murderous nor ignorant. They are stunningly normal, and I am saddened at the loss the rest of the world suffers by this deception. They are missing out on an entire group of intelligent, and yet starkly ordinary people. But I am also grateful, for the fog veiling me has lifted, and while some of it remains, I believe everyone has a little cloud they cannot extinguish. But I am glad to be rid of most of it, for it is unpleasant and heavy.

I smile at the woman until my cheeks hurt and she looks at me, amused. She laughs as she looks at me looking her. And then her baby is crying and she is occupied. I force my eyes to look anywhere else. My attention is refocused to my purpose, and I set away my plate and walk out of the extravagant dining hall. I put on my green army jacket over my sweater and take a deep breath, walking out. Today feels different. A sense of purpose fills me up and I feel peace envelope me like a warm blanket. The anxiousness comes later.

Chapter Sixteen

I go to the only bakery I know of. It is on the road to the Blue Mosque and the Grand Bazaar, and the day is beautiful so I make the trip by foot. The air is frigid but strong rays of sunshine hit my back and I feel its warmth.

I walk into the bakery, and immediately feel closed in. There are no tables in sight, but a staircase winds up into something unseen. There is one aisle that is crammed with a long line of locals. But the lighting is soft and pretty, and I inhale the gorgeous scent of bread, sweetness, cardamom, and spice. I smell the strong Turkish coffee before I see it across from me in an ornamented gold jug and tray, partially secluded by a big tall man with greying hair and two children. The baby boy clings to his pants and leans against him. The older girl pats his back with glowing excitement, and speaks in rushed Turkish jumble, pointing to the chocolates behind her.

Her hair is woven into a long braid, and her eyes are a striking green that I can spot from across the room.

He shakes his head, half listening. But he is smiling and he rubs the back of the little boy's head. Their clothes are old, dirty, and mismatched, but their love is tangible. I can see its glow, feel its warmth, and secretly, I crave it. I shuffle through my memories of childhood, trying to remember a time I felt a love like that firsthand. Brief, fleeting moments come to mind, but only when life was good and I had done something worthy of my parents' pride and attention. A part of me, the automatic ingrained part of me, reprimands this thought and I feel guilt swarm through me. I know my thoughts are correct. My family loves me, but not as much as I wished they did. Not as much as I needed them to.

The man gets his plastic bagged order, and he walks past me with two kids trailing past me. His face is grim even as he smiles, and the boy is crying. And I know then that no family is perfect, and no love is unconditional. Everything has terms. Everything has limits.

I reel my thoughts back from darker, deeper things. And then I think about the boy whom I'm to buy bread for. I think about where it will be, sitting there next to him. I don't expect him to eat it, or at least not all of it. He will wait until death is banging at his door, and then, and only then will he pull out this bread and eat a small portion of it. This thought saddens me, and makes me wonder if what I'm doing only delays the inevitable. That boy is going nowhere. This food I buy will run out. The jacket will be insignificant in harsher weather. The socks will get dirty and those too will never be enough. I could buy all the food and clothes I wanted, and it would never be enough. Nothing I ever do will ever be enough.

I buy the bread anyway. What else can I do?

Chapter Seventeen

The fruit stand man is gone. My heart sinks, as I miss his strange humor and warmth. He is replaced with a teenage boy who shouts to the pedestrians, holding up bagged bread and yelling prices. I walk up to him and he turns to me with a grin. I see a resemblance to the fruit stand man. Same long nose and moss green eyes. All Turkish locals are ridiculously attractive, and it makes me feel the unfair imbalance in the world.

"What you like? Bread very good," the boy tells me, holding up a bag of raisin bread and grinning, so much that his crooked teeth are on full display.

I attempt to smile back, and point to the fruit. "Actually, can I get some of the fruit?"

"Yes, yes! Five apple two lira, five banana two lira, and three orange one lira."

My palms sweat at the thought of bargaining, but I force myself to speak. "What if I get three apples, two oranges, and five bananas. Can you give me a lower price?" He laughs and looks at the fruit, as if the answers are written on the orange peels. Finally he looks up and says. "Okay okay, I give you all for four liras? Okay?"

I nod and he smiles at me, bagging the fruit in a thin plastic bag. I pull out the cash with caution since I brought too many big bills. And then I get my fruit, he wishes me well, and I walk away. My next stop is a clothes stall. I scribble out "shoes" from my list since I have no recollection of what the boy's feet looked like. But I go to a small shoe polishing stand, and I pay for three socks. Those are added to my already heavy bag, and my back aches but I silence the complaints in my head with the wails of a certain green eyed child.

I think about the toy and decide to buy one. I am unsure if it is really for the boy's pleasure or for my peace of mind. Either way, this silly gesture feels essential. And that is how I find myself in the Grand Bazaar for the second time in my life, and just as foundered by its massiveness and grandeur. The structure is entirely underground, save for a few stalls selling nuts and dried fruits at the descending staircase and entrance. The bazaar is miles long, composed of infinite small stores. There are a few chain stores, but the McDonald's chains of the world are wealthy countries unwilling to help. And even while it is the beginning of March, the place swarms with tourists from around the world, like an international, diverse beauty.

My feet stumble with the tight crowd. I awkwardly slip off my jacket, feeling hot in the heat of crammed bodies. I look at the people and at the shops. A few stick in my mind, like the stone jewelry stand run by a woman with a face veil. I also remember the soap stand I bought from last time. There is a leather products store. I try on a white leather jacket after much persuasion by a suave salesman. But it fits tight and looks unfitting with my pale skin and plain, woodsy clothing style. I am again forced to remember my sister and mother, and quickly take off the jacket and pass it to the shop owner, eager to go someplace else.

I end up at a kite shop, hidden in the corner between a dried herbs store and a rock collection stand. My feet take me inside, and there I find myself. I am surrounded by kites of all different shapes, sizes, and colors. They cover the brown murky walls and ceiling. As I often find myself in these stores, a man rushes to me and begins talking in broken English. He isn't smiling, which is a rare trait in this crowd. Every shop owner here looks like they just won the lottery, even when I say no. But this man is a skinny, surly grump. But it's okay, since I barely pay him attention.

Instead I look at the kites as my fingers delicately sweep the rubbery material across the walls. Yellow, blue, neon pink, green, black, white, gray… until one color blends into the next. The store is a whirlwind and I am lost. I try to hush the monsters in my head, but they climb out and claw at my heart. I remember my dad, the park, and lost childhood mornings trying to soak up the illusion of perfection in my life. I try not to notice my parents' favoring to my sister. My smart, perfect, freakishly clean sister. The girl who showers four times a day and organizes stationary first by size then by color. Her. Over me.

But now I am well past nine years old and my resolve to resist these thoughts has weakened, crumpled to dust. And I am left bearing the brunt of the truth. Except those mornings with the kites and the wind and my father… there was some truth to those moments, no matter how small. No matter how rationally insignificant, considering current events. They existed. And maybe that is why the loss of my past family hurts so deeply.

The shopkeeper comes close to my left shoulder and I tense, turning to face him.

"So you don't want two for one? Good price, heh," he tells me, looking slightly offended at my indifference towards him.

"No." I begin to leave, before I turn around. "Thank you," I say, as an afterthought. He doesn't call after me.

Chapter Eighteen

I go back to the kite store and settle on a sky blue modest-sized kite with brown string. The gift seems illogical, considering the boy resides in the city and he barely gets himself to eat food that is given to him. But I get it anyway, because it reminds me of my own parents. Who does that boy have to give him crazy, crappy gifts? My father may not have won any parenting awards, but at least he was present, mostly.

The kite shopkeeper's eyes go alight with brief delight at his success. I thank him again, out of habit, and then I am out for the second time. I look around me, at the hustle of the crowd and the shops, and the peculiar smell of soap and spice and leather. But I am tired of this scene, and I have things to do. I am soon out of the bazaar and feel the cool wind of the city tickle my skin. The bazaar is so crowded, body heat has kept me warm. But now I am shivering, so I put my jacket on awkwardly, with all these bags. My hands are heavy and cold and my back aches. But this all seems unimportant with my task at hand. I am still full from breakfast, but fatigue plagues me so I buy a small bag of dried nuts and fruits. Also, out of a strange and illogical insistence, I find myself in possession of roasted chestnuts. I try one for no apparent reason, but I have to force the small bite down my throat. Yes, the peculiar taste of this one thing is still not lost on me.

I walk down the same streets, feeling an odd sense of danger awaiting and continue my walk with cautious steps and darting looks around me. But I see nothing, and soon, my feet are back at regular pace. The city is particularly cold today, and harsh winds flap my jacket against me. Goosebumps run along my skin and I shiver. Then I see him as I always do, huddled loosely against an alley wall, staring blankly. Except this time, he is wearing the jacket and the scarf. It is properly tied too, and this surprises me. My feet carry me until I stand at his right and I smile instinctively. He looks up at me, and I am surprised at what I see. His eyes hold nothing but surprise and maybe a slight warmth. His lips are sealed shut as usu-al. But on the right corner of his face, there is big bruise that reaches his bleeding nose. And his blue lips and red face draw attention to the small cuts all the way up to the bottom of his eyelid.

My heart breaks. Slowly, slowly, then painfully, all at once.

Chapter Nineteen

Words spill out of me before I can stop them.

"What happened?" I ask him. He looks at me, blank, scared, and resigned. I'm scared he doesn't even care anymore. I'm scared that he has no reason to care. So I do the only thing I think of. I reach out my hand. There we are. He sits, curled up away from me. And I hover over him with burning knees and an outstretched hand. I stay like this, even after my knees tremble from my weight and my arm aches from waiting. But I stay, waiting.

And then a miracle happens. He takes my hand. His rough, small, frozen trembling hand briefly leaves a feather light touch on my palm. And I see it in his eyes. He begs me to save him. And I try. I grasp onto his hand the moment his fingers reach mine. And I then I get up, hands still tied together, and I tug at him. He looks at me, right into my eyes. And I am unsure of what he sees, but the next thing I see is him stiffly reaching for the grocery bag behind him, the bag I gave him. And then he takes my hand, squeezes it, and gets up. He stands.

My awe for this boy comes later. But the warmth does

not. A glow inside me sparks the moment this boy accepted my hand. And it burns brighter from there.

I flag down a cab with one hand, but keep him firmly grasped in the other. I can't lose him now. But something tells me he doesn't want to leave.

I let him get in first, and then climb into the back. The driver looks at me with skepticism, but I ignore it. "Radisson Hotel, please." The man nods, and the car jerks into motion, like all the cabs here do. This is the first time I sit in a car in Istanbul, and don't notice the city around me. All I notice is that boy. I catch slight glimpses of him, but quickly look away when I see he stares at me. That's how the first half of the drive goes. He burns holes in the side of my head with his blank, curious, sad gaze. Finally, he looks out the window and I feel my shoulders sink and let out tension I didn't realize I held.

Finally, we reach the hotel. I pay the driver and climb out of the rusty car. I look at the boy, and for the second time that night, I offer the boy my hand.

"I'm Penelope." The words fumble but they are out now, lingering in the air. The boy catches them. He looks down, then up, takes my hand, and speaks to me.

"Ameer."

I smile at his voice. It is rough and low, like it hasn't been used in years. And in the midst of the sadness and darkness in his eyes, I see a thin layer of the ice around him melt.

Chapter Twenty

The sound of the door closing sounds loud in the quiet room. I wince. I kick off my shoes, and see Ameer looking at me. He looks uncomfortable. I surrender my hands above my shoulders.

"It's okay. You're okay."

He nods, slowly. I go to the coffee maker counter and get the ice bucket.

"I'm going to go fill up the ice bucket, okay?" I point to the bucket. "I'll be right back."

I pull open the door, and the wheezing door sounds loud to me again. I shut it and walk down the empty hotel hallway. I find a small room with bright white lights and fumble with the ice maker until my bucket is full. Then I hurry back, my heart beating erratically. I fear I will return to an empty room. But when I slide my key card in and reach for the doorknob, he is sitting on the floor against a wall. I stay as far as possible from the door so he doesn't feel trapped in. And then I grab the smallest towel I can find in the bathroom. I sit on the hard, brown carpeted floor with him and try to smile. The task proves harder than I imagined.

I fill the towel with chunks of ice, and wrap it up. My hands betray me. I feel anxious, and the boy's - Ameer's - anxiety is tangible in the stiff, stale air. Still, I take a deep breath, and gently press the ice to his face. He flinches, but remains seated. His eyes stay on my face. Mine stay on his bruises. I busy myself with the ice, because if I don't, then I have to focus on him, and I don't think I could handle that yet.

After a few minutes with ice held to his face, Ameer gently moves himself from the ice. I understand his signal, and throw out the remaining ice and toss the wet towel onto the bathroom floor. I see blood on the towel, and my heart squeezes. I take another deep breath, and stumble to my suitcase, pulling out my first aid kit. I find a bandaid and my magic ointment from India. It stinks like rotten eggs, but it is a small price to pay for the miracles it works. I sit on the floor again and sit the bandaid on the floor, and open up the squeeze bottle. Its pungent smell hits me, but I squeeze some onto my finger, and then, breath held, rub it onto the open wound. He is still staring at me. And then I stick on the bandaid.

By the time I come back from throwing away the wrappers, Ameer is lying on the floor. I fill up a glass with water and get my banana bread from the mini fridge. I cut off a big slice with the plastic knife by the sugar packets, put it on a napkin, and set it next to him. I tap his shoulder gently, like a hesitating caress, and his eyes pop open. He stares at me then looks at my offering. He sits up, and looks at me once more, as if asking for permission. I nod at him, smiling. He nods at me, like a silent thank you. I smile at him, and sit next to him on the floor. He scratches his head, like he has been, and gingerly picks up the glass. He drinks it in one gulp. And then he picks up the whole piece of bread with his small, dirt covered hands and stuffs as much as he can into his mouth. He doesn't bother swallowing one bite before stuffing in another chunk. When he is done, wet crumbs coat his mouth. He doesn't bother wiping them off. I don't know why that bothers me, but it does. Badly. Still, I ignore it. I offer him more bread, but he shakes his head. I am about to cut him another piece anyway, but his head gently falls to the ground and his eyes close. I sigh, and take the napkin and plate from the floor, and set them on the table.

There is a sofa in the lounge area, where we sit now. The bed is on the other side of the room, and the bathroom is wedged in the middle, across from the coat closet. The boy- Ameer- scratches his head again, deeply and for a long time. I wonder when was the last time that boy had a shower. And with his body and head against that filthy brick wall... a shudder runs down my spine. I wouldn't be surprised if he has lice. No one attacks their scalp that way. I remember in fourth grade, this girl, Mindy, I think, had this perfect blonde hair that reached the top of her thighs. I would've been insanely jealous of it if it wasn't for the sheen of grease that made her head shine like an oiled croissant. I remember thinking that she looked like one of those cars in the commercials, that sparkle in the light. We were playing together in the playground, and she tackled me to the floor in a competitive, very politicized game of tag. We sort of tumbled in the dirt together, until the teacher, Mr. Simmons, pulled us apart. One week later, my sister screamed about a bug in my head. I had lice. It was the worst thing in the world.

I decide to take care of those little critters. But tonight, they would have to wait. This boy needs rest. And I need my

Property Brothers.

Chapter Twenty One

I nudge Ameer's shoulder. He doesn't budge. I nudge him once more, but to no avail. I resort to a tap on the head. His eyes pop open and an alarmed, frightened look overshadows the sleepiness. I feel guilty for waking him up in the first place. And then I feel my bottom sore from the hard ground.

"Take the bed. I'll sleep on the couch."

The alarm from his eyes is replaced by an innocent confusion. His eyebrows scrunch up and he tilts his head to the side, rubbing his eyes. I almost pinch his cheeks. Thank the Lord that I stop myself. That would've been sure to make him run out the door. I realize I'm grinning before I consciously allow it. I motion to the bed with my hands, and then point to myself and then to the couch. He nods in understanding, but shakes his head.

"Come on." He shakes his head once more, eyes drooping. I laugh, and his eyes pop open too. I'm not sure who's more surprised.

This he seems to understand, since he almost smiles back. Or maybe he doesn't. Maybe he's realizing what a crazy lady he's gone with.

I poke him on the shoulder, and he smiles at me and it feels like all is right with the world, even when everything spins out of control. Ameer is living proof of that. But the truth seems irrelevant right now.

As they always have been, Ameer's movements are slow and stiff like new leather. Finally he makes his way to the bed. I rush to pull off the comforters and try to feel useful by arranging the pillows. And then he collapses onto the bed, scratching his head again. His body sinks into the bed, but he doesn't move a muscle. I hear him sigh for a long, slow moment. And then he is gone, eyes shut, mouth open, still and silent. With featherlight touches, I pull his arms out from under his body and untangle his awkwardly placed legs. Then I let my fingertips rest on his shoulder, just for a second. And then I am out, and let out a breath I was not aware I was holding.

I try to soften the thud of my footsteps on my way to the bathroom. I shut the door with caution. Only when the door is shut and locked do I turn on the light. I let out another breath. My shoulders sink further into my chest. I stare at the woman in the mirror and I am at a loss. I do not recognize the girl blinking at me, mouth open.

Most of my hair sits at the base of my neck in a loose ponytail. The rest is a frizzy mess around my face. My hunched and aching stomach throb in a tense, strange way. The way it hurt after my first job interview for the local coffee shop in Charlottesville. My eyes are wide and glassy. My brown eyes have turned to a liquefied amber color, like sunlight drifting through autumn leaves, while my hands hang at my sides. I feel like I am hanging from a thread, about to fall into uncertain suspension, and a very possible doom. But I not ready. I am not ready to fall, to land or to crash. Somehow, I don't think the universe cares about what I am ready for.

Life happens to people. People don't make life happen.

And I am not ready for life to happen to me. Not again. Not now, never. But it will. Of this, I am sure.

Chapter Twenty Two

I sit on the bathroom floor tiles against the door without regard to time. My knees shake, up and down, like they always do whenever I am nervous or in extreme pain. I'm not sure which one it is this time. My heart hurts, and my head feels like they carry the weight of one thousand bricks. My breathing is growing ragged. I draw in short shallow breaths and it becomes shorter and shallower until I am panting like a dog begging for water. I slide down to the floor. Some part of my brain, maybe the part ingrained into me by my sister shrieks at all the germs I am currently bathing in. But this voice is swiftly silenced by a daunting, more pressing matter. I am unsure of what this matter is right now.

Goosebumps cover my skin and I shiver from the freezing floor. My back trembles and my teeth chatter. And then the thoughts rush at me like a freight train. I stupidly bang my head against the floor. It stings and throbs, so I have no logical explanation for repeating my actions. The second bang hurts more, but it throbs into a headache rather than a sharp sting. The coolness feels kind of nice on my head, so I rest my right cheek against the floor. My teeth bang against each other a little harder.

I stay like this for longer than I care to admit, before

the logical voice in my head finally rolls her eyes at me and tells me to pull myself together. And then she's gone in a poof, and I am forced to figure out the "how" part alone, with my emotion riddled, crazy, partly broken brain.

Step one: get off that filthy floor. I pull my head up first, and then my knees. And then I push my cold, possibly germ-riddled body off the floor and into standing position. I look at myself, disgusted with what I see. I shake these thoughts away, literally, and splash cold water onto my face. I scrub my skin with a rough towel that smells like bleach, chlorine, and pears. My face stays like that, buried in a hotel towel with a strange homeless boy sleeping on my bed. I shake my head, and toss the big towel next to the sopping bloody one. And then I shut off the lights, unlock the heavy door, and push it open. It creaks loudly, like an old grump moaning. I close it, and with a disappointed sigh, head for the couch. Step two was supposed to be to shower and get changed. But I forget about the chronology as soon as I hit the couch. I can hear Ameer's abrupt, rhythmic snores from here. When that boy is awake, he acts like fragile broken glass. But when he is asleep, he sounds like a lion.

I lie down, unceremoniously kicking my legs up on the armrest. And then I think. I think about my family, my job, my house... I think about home. My heart tugs, not because I miss home, but because I don't. And something tells me the feeling is mutual. All I miss are my baby blue bed, my coffee, and my clothes. Nothing else. Not my sister (that one I am not so shocked by), not my father, my acquaintances. I have very few friends to miss. Most are people I pass time with, people I am forced to deal with.

And then I think about everything here. My heart doesn't tug this time; it squeezes. Painfully. The children I see on my route to the same streets every morning. The buildings. The Blue Mosque, and that fountain that sits right in front of it. The roasted chestnuts I still have no taste for. The Grand Bazaar. The locals, especially those handsome salesmen. The food. And Ameer.

Leaving Ameer. Oh God.

I am unsure of how to make sense of the pain my heart feels at this thought, since I have known him for an insignificant time. I only learned his name a couple hours earlier. I'm not sure he even trusts me, and I have no difficulty believing I will wake up tomorrow and see an empty bed, with no trace of him. No sign he was ever here.

Maybe it is because we have so much in common. He may be a homeless Syrian boy while I am a privileged American with wealthy parents. But he has no parents; I lost my mother. We don't trust easily. We suffer in silence. We want to quit, but we don't. Or at least I hope we have that in common. I hope that boy holds on, even if only by a thread. The world doesn't deserve someone like him, but I hope he stays anyway.

I desperately hope so.

I may be well into my twenties, but I feel so small right now, like a child. And I can't help but think what if. What if I never went back? Would anyone care? Would I care?

What if I stayed?

Chapter Twenty Three

I wake up with an aching back and a heavy head. My head rests awkwardly against the couch armrest, and my neck is bent over. My legs drape unceremoniously over the opposite armrest and I have to get my arms out of a strange tangled mess of limbs. I sit up and rub my temples, but both things only exacerbate my symptoms. I continue to massage my head anyway, because that's what I've seen people do. Consider me a follower.

And then something clicks. The room is too silent, too still. I automatically know something is wrong, and I jump up to stand. My head gets worse and the hotel room spins around for a few seconds, but I stagger around until I reach the bed. He's gone. The room seems so unchanged, I wonder if last night was a dream. Some twisted movie my lonely heart conjured up. But then I look at the side table and the bathroom. I see the napkin in the wastebasket, and the glass is washed, dried, and set perfectly next to the coffee maker. The dirty towels are neatly folded next to the sparkling sink. A pretty useless move. But this is Ameer saying thank you. With no chance to reply.

I take one look at the cleaned areas and I know he is grateful. But I don't want him to be grateful; I want him to be here. I can't help a mini eruption of frustration explode in my chest. I'm mad at myself for not waking up and stopping him, mad at him for leaving.

I sit on the bed and think about what I am supposed

to do now. What is the protocol for situations like these? Do I go after him? Do I forget about him altogether? I feel insecure and I don't like it.

My mother used to say that when you don't know what you want, think about your ideal life. Where are you? Who are you with? What are you doing? Before Istanbul, before Ameer, I thought my perfect life was in a quaint home somewhere away from dad and Abby. I saw myself with a husband and a few kids, driving a minivan to my boys' soccer games, and writing articles for the Post or the Times as freelance. But now... now I don't know. I don't know if I want to settle for what everyone expects me to do. What I expect myself to do. I just don't know. I want to have a family, I want to be part-time journalist full time mother. I'm just not sure I want to do that yet.

I don't know if that boy is my future, but he symbolizes something so much bigger than just one person. Something bigger than any one of us. And I think if I let go of him, I'll be letting go of my dream.

I grab my boots.

Chapter Twenty Four

My appetite is gone, replaced by a rush of adrenaline, but my head feels heavy and things begin to spin. I stand in front of the bread man, the one I am familiar with, and give him money for a bag of apples I can pass out to the children.

But he stares at me with concerned eyes, unconcerned about my drooping hand with his money.

"You good? No food, huh?" he asks in his effortlessly charming voice.

I muster a smile at this. "I'm okay. Here's your money." The concern in his face transforms into a resolute, stubbornness. I would know; I have become well-acquainted with that look in the mirror.

"You no eat, I no take money."

My smile grows. Such care from a stranger warms me in a fuzzy, loving way. My heart goes out to this man. "I will, I will."

He shakes his head. "No, no. You tricking. You no eat." Now I am laughing, from the purest form of happiness, of peace. Even if it is only fleeting. The memory of this moment, of this man is more than I can ask for. More than I can expect. "Bread? You like? Eh, you like." He fumbles with the knot of the bag, eventually ripping the thing open. He hands me the torn bag, and motions with his head for me to eat.

"Well, thank you… but now?"

He looks at me with raised eyebrows. "Hah, yes."

I smile, and move to the side of his stall, awkwardly standing for a moment, before I notice him watching me, with crossed arms and a pointed look. I try not to notice how beautiful his ice blue eyes are, but my brain is unstoppable. So I look down, and busy myself with ripping off a chunk of bread. My hands fumble with his eyes burning a hole into my side. And then I am shoving sweet, honey banana bread down my throat. It tastes like heaven and I forget about him watching me. I finish a third of the loaf by the time I am done. I wipe self-consciously at the crumbs that line my mouth, and the stickiness of the honey and banana stains my hand, so I rub it on the top of my pants, feeling very much like a child. But the bread man is smiling- no, grinning at me. I smile back without thinking, and thank him again, handing him a wad of cash, adding extra for the bread. He laughs this time, and he is back to the carefree man I am so used to seeing. I wave him goodbye, and he laughs again, greeting me with loud, Turkish words.

"Kendine iyi bak," he says. I assume it means goodbye.

Chapter Twenty Five

I walk to the street corner. On my way, I imagine what I will see. A crowd of people, each in their own worlds. The same shoe shops. Cobblestone, hilly streets. Ameer sits in a valley. I see the restaurant in my mind. And then I see Ameer. In the same clothes I gave him, looking a little fresher.

But the sight that greets me is starkly different. In actuality, mostly everything is the same as I predicted. The restaurant, the road, the hills, the shops. But the important piece, the one that matters to me… Ameer. He stands in the same place he used to curl up. He has a flimsy grocery bag in his hands, and he shakes it at people, asking for money. I recognize the bag as the same one I had given him. He is begging. I am aware of how strange it is to feel proud, but I do. Feel proud. Begging is not a respectable job. People shame beggars. I used to, until today. Until Ameer. Because if he is begging, he cares. He cares to get money, to eat. To survive. He cares and my heart soars to the skies.

Usually, my feet lead the way, and the next thing I know, I am standing in front of this boy, crouching next to him. But this time my movements toward him. Are deliberate. Planned. I may not have a plan yet, but I plan to make one. I don't know what I'm doing with my life. But I do know I haven't done much so far. I have given nothing to this world. And that needs to change, and I plan to start with this boy in front of me. I have never cared about a stranger as much as I do for this boy. And I plan to do something about it. Better late than never, right?

His eyes are unfocused at the midst of the crowd. And then they sweep over me, zooming back to me. They widen, like a deer caught in headlights. I pause. I see surprise, skepticism. But I don't see fear, so I keep walking. I feel each foot move in front of the next. I feel the stickiness on my hands. I feel my boots crunch miniature stones. I feel the wind caress my cheeks and dry my hands. And I feel his eyes on me. I feel everything.

His hands freeze, then fall to his sides, his right hand clutching the plastic bag. I make my feet move until I am standing in front of him. I don't know what to say. I don't speak Arabic and he doesn't know a lick of English. I assume as much. I shake myself out of my reverie and search through my bag for a peace offering. I come up empty handed. Then I remembered my wallet, and pull that out. I give him all I have except a couple odd singles to get a ride back to the hotel, or at least to an exchange ATM. But when I look up to slip the money into his- my- bag, he shakes his head and smiles at me. Tingles shoot down my spine. I am about to smile back, when I look down at his hands.

The kite. It is still wrapped in plastic, but the tape has been peeled open, and it is folded oddly and without uniform. He has played with it. I stand there, speechless at who this boy is becoming. I see the excitement in his eyes dimming and I realize how I must look. Gaping mouth, wide eyes; I probably look like I want to run away. I grin at him, and some of the warmth returns. He looks vulnerable like that, with his beggar's bag in one hand and a kite in another. Ameer is an anomaly. Part grown, part child. And even if today's reality cannot be his true reality, today, the child will be who he really is. Even if tomorrow, this preteen boy has to beg for his survival, today he will be free.

I motion with my hands if he wants to fly the kite, and his smile disappears. He looks down at the grocery bag, swinging in the wind. I see his hand tighten around the tearing handles. Hanging by a thread. My eyes burn and I take the bag from him, tie it loosely, and push it into my bag. People look at me like they're wondering if they need to beat up a woman. But Ameer smiles at me and their worry fades into skepticism. But no one stops us; they don't care enough for that. And then we walk to the benches. And the world fades into the background.

Chapter Twenty Six

We reach the Blue Mosque, the Hagia Sophia, and I rethink my decisions. I have never liked attention, and I see no one else flying their kites. And Ameer and I are quite an odd pairing. A grown, white woman who is clearly a tourist, and a Syrian runaway boy in torn clothes and a dirty face. And lice. I pray that I get a chance to take care of that.

My doubt fades into the background, much like the people around us after I take one look at the boy next to me.

His eyes are focused on nothing but the clear blue sky. He smiles boyishly and looks at me shyly.

"Well, come on now. Open it!" I motion with my hands frantically. He smiles down at the bag. I don't think he realizes how happy he looks right now. I make no mention of it. But a moment like this deserves to be preserved, and I consider a selfie. But that will come later. Right now, we fly.

He opens the package like it is made of glass and then sets the packaging on the bag. But the wind tosses it around, and I catch it mid air, stuffing that in my bag too, right next to the plastic bag. Ameer sees it in my purse, and the brightness in his face dims, but only for a second. And then this new kid is back as he trains his attention on the kite. He fumbles until it is unfolded. Then he stares at the spool of yarn unsurely. I smile and walk over. I show him how to let it into the air. It is a baby beginner's kite, but his inexperience make it a challenge. I help him get it up and soon it is in the sky.

And then it kerplunks back down to solid ground, and I laugh hysterically. He giggles and we clasp our arms together, shaking. I feel people watching us, but I almost want them to see. I want them to see this boy who has been through so much and yet is transformed by a simple kite. I admire this child so much. His laughter may be young, but his shabby appearance tells a different story. And then I see those children I gave the fruit to just paces away from me, and I feel their laughter as much as I hear it. And I want to applaud these children of Syria, these misfits. They have nowhere to belong, no one to call their own, no place to call home. And yet... yet there they are. Running mindlessly, filling the air with sweet laughter.

Then they see me and they run to me. A chorus of Arabic greetings are spoken to me and I smile back, letting out a hoarse, "hello." And then they see Ameer, half hidden behind me. I step back which forces him to greet them. He nods his head and smiles politely. One of the girls shakes his shoulder and the kids almost yank him into their circle, and they chat in Arabic, tossing questions at him left and right. I hear him say things like "Ameer", and something with the street he stays on. I smile at them, feeling a little left out. But a warmth seeps into the rest of me.

The teenage girl in a bright pink sequin hijab stands next to me. The gaudy, mismatched outfit looks nothing like her, but I suppose she's lucky to have it anyway. If she notices me giving her a once over, she makes no mention of it. I try to make up for my rude behavior by offering her my hand. She takes it firmly.

"Penelope."

She gives me a small polite smile. Though I suspect it is more for my benefit than hers. "Ma Salaama. Jameela."

I grin at her. "Pretty name."

She laughs lightly, for a fleeting moment. "Means pretty."

I smile at her. "Suits you. You are very pretty."
She laughs bashfully. But she is. Pretty, I mean. She is. Her face is a clear white and her eyes are a beautiful, deep green, covered with long, curved eyelashes. Her light brown eyebrows are perfectly, and naturally shaped. And her small lips suit her oval face perfectly. Even though her sunken cheeks are too small to be healthy, anyone with working eyes can see her perfectly defined cheekbones.

And she lives on the streets. I can only get a similar look after hours of painful preparation.

But she has a bold aura that is just as attractive. She smiles kindly, but I know with certainty that she can just as easily turn on me if she had to. She stands tall and while her arms are crossed, they look just as intimidating at the rest of her.

I cannot help but wonder what these children's stories are. What gave Jameela her strong stance, or Ameer his sad smile? Or the three other children, what gave them their carefree look? I suspect that is at least partially the result of Jameela's efforts.

I also wonder what makes Jameela wear that pink scarf.

I know it is a religious custom from Islam, made to keep women modest. But why would anyone bother with something like religion when they don't even have a home, and three children to look after? She is either incredibly stupid, or incredibly faithful. Sometimes, I wonder what the difference is.

I think back to when my mother died and how I dealt with it. I curled up in bed, didn't leave my room, and got angry at my dad, the man who had just lost his wife as I had lost my parent. I quit. I quit on my family, my friends, my school. On life, in general. And what does this girl do, when she not only loses both her parents, her friends, but her way of life? Her home, her shops, her school? She takes three kids and chases after them in a strange city, in a new world. I wonder what I would have done in her situation. And then I stop, since that train of thought is destined to crash and burn. And she's still wearing that scarf. She didn't give up on God, either.

Chapter Twenty Seven

Night is coming. My feet ache and sting from blisters, and my arms are sore from repeatedly getting the kite back in the air. I'm sure Ameer has many talents, but kite flying is not one of them. I didn't mind, though. I didn't mind at all. This orphan kid who went from a war zone to a brand new city, homeless, was happy. Anyone could see it in his eyes and his smile, hear it in his laughter, and feel it from the heat it generates around him, like a burning fire people huddle around on a cold, relentless night.

The other children huddle around Ameer, and eventually, he passes the kite wordlessly to the small, bony girl next to him. And then she is running, keeping the kite high in the air. The air draws energy, and the kite flaps and rises with the girl's assistance. And then another kid gets the kite and the kite falls and the children scream with laughter. There were at least seventeen children, and every single one of them looked entranced by a toy that cost me less than a cheeseburger back home. I sit on the bench for a while, but an unexplainable energy, a ball of flames bursts inside me, and sitting makes me squirm with anxiety. So I stand next to one of the small girls, trying to feel useful. But I just stand there. Every few minutes, the children look at me and grin with this adoring, sweet look in their eyes, that I feel like crying and grinning all at once. And then they would offer me the kite, yelling in Arabic for me to take it. But I always shook my head and smiled, urging them with my hands for them to take it. The kite has fallen eleven times in the past two hours we have been here. I counted.

But now night is coming. The sky has gone from a bright blue and rays of yellow, to an enchanting crimson. Oddly, it reminds me of my mother's cranberry sauce, like a fleeting candle light in a black room. And then it leaves me, and I am back to thinking about the children, the kite, and the nagging thought in the back of my head; the lice. Most of these kids scratch their heads with their long filthy nails, and

I wish I could bring them all with me, but I can't. I wordlessly tell them we should go, and I expect them to wave goodbye, but they don't. Instead, the girl with the long braided black hair pushes the kite into my hands. The children laugh and cheer me on.

I feel the plastic, grimy handle and I smell the city air. It is not a smell I associate with those trips with my dad, and the texture rubbing against my palms is starkly different. But something in me overflows with nostalgia, and I tighten my grip and attempt a few deep breaths. And then I awkwardly stumble backwards to get the kite back. A little to the left. No, right. And then back. Farther. Farther.

The world simultaneously fades into the background and keeping the kite soaring becomes my most intense object of focus. I hear the children's happiness near me, but I pay little attention to it. I feel eyes on me, but it does not register. Nothing does, except the sweet sound of wind, the familiar chill of April air, and the kite overhead. A spot of blue in an infinite cranberry sky.

No matter what happens after, for one brief moment, I am infinite.

Chapter Twenty Eight

Ameer grasps the kite with his fingertips and swings his arms in a newfound energy. His lips turn up in an unconscious manner, and his body sways with the wind. So different from the stiff, sad child yesterday and the day before, and the day before that.

We stop by a small pharmacy. The Turkish letters outside flicker and the inside is grimy. The air is cheap and the tiles are unwashed. But I find the lice kit, I pay, and I go out. We continue our walk back to the hotel. My body aches and I wonder why we don't take the train. Maybe the mundaneness of it would ruin tonight's magic. But that is already lost, broken. The kite came back down, and so did reality. Only one landed softly. Even Ameer's eyebrows furrow and he looks like he is back to being tense in thought. For some reason, that hurts.

We get to the hotel and ride the elevator up with a young British couple. The husband doesn't notice our presence, but the woman looks from me to Ameer and then back. She does this twice, before looking up at the ceiling of the elevator like it is a work of art. And then she looks at me and frowns. I can almost see the thoughts running through her head. What is a tourist woman doing with a dirty street child? A refugee?

I hear a voice in my head slap me over the head for my snootiness. But I can't help it. Well, I don't try. Sometimes, one gaze is sufficient without words. So I roll my eyes at my feet, and I feel her frowning again. But then the elevator dings, and they climb off. Ameer and I ride up in silence and I feel him looking at me. I turn to look back, and see so many unspoken words he wants to let out. A similar feeling my own gut stirs. A language barrier is exactly that: a barrier. There is so much I want to tell this boy, and assumingly, so much he wants to tell me. But they hang in the air. No one grabs at them. But maybe that is a good thing. Words create doubts. Maybe if we could speak, Ameer would have never taken the bet and trusted me when I led him here that first time, and then to the kite. And here, now.

We get off the elevator and I brought him to the room, swiping my card in. We go in and I sink into the couch. My energy drains, and there is nothing more that I want then to collapse right into this sofa. But I force myself up and open the pharmacy plastic bag, pulling out the lice kit. I nod my head at an awkwardly awaiting Ameer by the door, and lead him to the bathroom.

I get a white bath towel, and turn to Ameer. He nods at me, and I give him the towel. But he just stands there and questions me with a look. I put the towel on the sink counter and I pull out the lice kit. I show him the packaging, and I see him struggle with the Turkish writing. And then he nods while reading. But he looks up at me.

"For you?"

I laugh at this. "No. You," I say and point to his head that he is currently scratching.

"No, no. Me-" and then gives me the Arabic thumbs up and I smile, shaking my head.

"No. No you aren't. You keep scratching." I bring my hands to my scalp and make a scratching motion.

He resists with gestures and loose words, but I persist until he finally quits. He takes the towel with a small smile, and drapes it on his back and shoulders. Then he ducks his head under the sink until his whole face is wet. I pass him a hand towel and he pats his face with it. He looks dazed. This is probably the first time he has washed his head with water from a faucet. I try not to linger on this thought, and I busy myself with the lice kit. I rip open the package and get the instructions, even though I have done that many times. I don't want to mess up.

I grab the small bottle of the shampoo and twist it open. The pungent smell of chemical and bleach hits me and pollutes the room. I pull on the provided gloves, and then squeeze some of the yellow, gel-like paste into my hands. Ameer is tall for his age, so my arms extend up to reach his head. He sees my arms in the mirror we are facing, and he crouches to the floor and sits on his knees. I smile at his intuition and his care.

The rubbered hands massage his scalp and roots. My hands ache by the time I am done, and I leave him in the bathroom after washing my hands. My feet lead me to the couch, and I sink into it again. I mean to only sleep twenty minutes, while we wait for the shampoo to do its work. But the next time my eyes open, Ameer is walking over to me with washed hair, wearing only pants and a towel he grips over himself. When his hair is combed. Ameer looks at me with a certain praise, but he says nothing on the couch next to me. He just reaches for my hand, and squeezes. He doesn't let it go, even when his grip loosens after he falls asleep next to me.

I don't let him go, either.

Chapter Twenty Nine

The morning after, order returns. I wake up to an empty room, and I learn an hour later that Ameer returns to his street space. I stay in my world; he returns to his. The day passes without my consent. I eat leftover banana bread, skipping the buffet. And then I get a cab to Ameer. I see him there, begging for money in a different plastic bag this time. And then I fumble with my purse, and I see the wrinkled plastic bag filled with change. I think about running to him and giving him his bag. For the bag, I think. Just one last time.

But that is the problem. It won't be one last time. He'll run out of food, or winter will get harsh. And every time I close my eyes, I imagine myself seeing him dead. Lying untouched on the side of the street, until someone with an ounce of decency calls the police and they carry him away.

The thought, the picture… it feels so real that I turn and walk away from Ameer on trembling legs and blurry eyes. And then my body endures the sudden exhaustion of anxiety, of worrying, until I find myself slumped on a park bench where we flew that kite. Where I met those children, and they met me. Where Ameer and all the children of Syria stole another part of my heart. Another part of me.

I sit there until an old gentleman taps me on the shoulder and asks if I'm okay in broken English. I give him an equally crooked smile and nod my head, thanking him for asking. And then I force myself up on my feet, and I walk to the Blue Mosque, since admission is free.

A magnificent, round chandelier hands in the middle. The stained glass is painted with images of Jesus, but there is a painting of the Islamic crescent on the wall. There is a cross right next to it. And then there are tourists, selfie sticks, and red restricting rope. A combination of what was a church, and then a mosque, and now a tourist attraction. I remember my history teacher in high school used to say that history is fluid, and it is very much alive. I feel its warm breath on me as I look around me. Through the years, history had its winners and losers. It was a constant fight for dominance. For the upper hand. First, the Christians won. And then the Muslims won. And then it was abandoned altogether.

Maybe this is what I am so afraid of. I'm sure the Muslims never daydreamed about abandoning their dominance here, in this very structure. They saw themselves as everlasting, ever growing. And that is what I do with Ameer. I imagine that I will go back home, and years later, I will see him working some campus job at a local college in America. Or I'll see him on the news, in a refugee program in Canada. And then I wonder about the other futures. The unpleasant possibilities, that are endless. But whenever I wake up to an empty hotel room, I always expect that everything will turn out okay.

But life is a roll of the dice, and more often than people like to admit, our daydreams don't come true. But I don't want to leave Ameer's future up to chance. Maybe he'll raise enough money on the streets, and he will be okay. But I am terrified that my dreams are all my fantasies will ever be. I see him, dead on the streets. Or beaten in an alleyway. Or frozen outside some shelter. Or at a refugee camp. Forever. I see him grow old there, alone, and die, forgotten, without a trace. And I am even more terrified that these nightmares will be more than just my pessimistic imagination after sleep deprivation and a rough day.

I leave the Blue Mosque and hail a taxi. Tonight, I will secure Ameer's future. Tonight, this ends.

Chapter Thirty

The sun is still shining bright in a cloudless sky when I greet the big, grand door of the restaurant, down the alleyway. I walk in with hunched shoulders, sweaty clothes, and shallow breaths from my long walk from the mosque. I walk up to a server who carries a tray holding steaming, beautifully arranged dishes. He shoots me an impatient smile, and nods his head. I state a name.

"No come," he tells me, and then holds up five fingers, and then two. Then he points to the once grand clock, that is now rusted and outdated. I nod my head at him and grin. "Thank you," I say. He smiles at me, but I am already walking over to an empty booth big enough for four. Seven o'clock. That means I have over an hour to kill. I cringe at the phrase that runs through my head. Time to kill.

I could leave and return at the time, but paranoia of losing my chance keeps me seated. That, and my aching feet. My head is heavy and I am drained of energy. So I order a mint lemonade (after much persistence). The glass is tall and coated in condensation The lemonade is citrusy and it cuts through the heaviness in my stomach. And the nerves. The mint is real and I see flecks of forest green in the yellow when I swirl my straw. I entertain myself by patterning my swirls with the white and red striped straw. By 6:30, the glass is half empty, along with my patience. My heartbeat is quickening and I shake my right leg continuously. An old local man looks at me like I am deranged. I pinch my knee and force myself to focus on the tension of waiting. I was never very good at this part.

I release a long breath and imagine it as tension. My shoulders sink from their upright position and I look through my bag, but I find nothing for entertainment. I have a pen but no paper. So I resume to shaking my leg. I convince myself of hunger, and pick up the menu from the other side of the table. I wave down a cheaply dressed waiter, and order a small chicken shawarma. He asks if I want fries, but I shake my head in total refusal. Turkish fries are usually an injustice. They are tasteless and soggy. My order comes soon. I see steam rise from the scratched, old white plate. The wrap is covered in foil, and I tear at the top and bite. The chicken is juicy and flavorful, the pickles are soggy but citrusy, and the garlic paste adds a punch to the otherwise simple flavors. By the time 7:00 rolls around, my glass and plate are empty, the bill is paid, and I am satisfied. I stand up in a haste, eager to meet him. I walk out of the restaurant at 7:10, and I see him standing there, waving at people. No one pays him any attention. He sees me before I can get to him, and he waves with a warm smile.

He stops advertising and turns to give me his undivided attention. I reach him with nervousness and fear. But mostly, there is hope. One look at this man's smile, at his fluttering grey-black hair, at his worn hands, his ironed, worn clothes. One look and I lose my doubt. Something definite and dangerous replaces it: certainty. I am sure this will work. But time will tell. As it always does, soundlessly.

Chapter Thirty One

I stand paces away from him. From my solution. From a godsend. For Ameer. He just doesn't know it yet. I lessen the distance between us, and my heart races at the prospects of tonight. My palms are sweaty. My confidence in the success of our near future is slipping. But I take a deep breath and let the words tumble out into the open, polluted air.

"I need to talk to you."

Mr. Ghanzali's smile becomes wary and concerned. Like he is contemplating if I am either dangerous or in danger. Neither will end well for him. He knows this, yet he nods in cautious acceptance. I expect him to ask if something is wrong, and he does. I evade his question and repeat my request.

"Okay," he says. "I take an early break today. Come with me."

We walk together inside. The air between us, in our

own world, is tense and awkward, and I want to leave. But I have waited too long to simply walk away. And there is too much at stake. There is a boy on the line today, and for that, I will not run out of cowardice.

He motions for me to sit at a table. I preferred a booth, because they are casual. Relaxed. Although I suppose that is exactly why a metal table is better. It provides distance between us, and the lighting is harsher here. The lightheartedness, the gentleness of this place seems misplaced and unfitting, for what is about to go down. Still, I sit in a torn cushioned metal chair.

My knee is shaking unstoppably by the time the man returns and sits across from me. He rests his clasped hands on the table, and I see all his playfulness disappear. I swallow, hard, but I force myself to still my leg. I clear my throat, and then I begin.

"Thank you for agreeing to meet with me. I know it cost you your work break."

I'm stalling and he knows it. I see it in his unwavering expression. "Of course. Now, what is the problem? Did you get hurt?"

"No, I'm fine." Here goes nothing. One more deep breath, and then I begin.

"A couple of days ago, I met this boy, Ameer. He was homeless, a refugee from Syria. I gave him food and clothes a couple times, whenever I passed him on my way to the Blue Mosque. Except, one night when I passed by him, he was slumped on the ground. He was covered in bruises and blood.

So I took him to my room and fixed him up. He slept there for a night."

At this, Mr. Ghanzali tilts his head and gives me a, "what are you up to" look. My cheeks heat up at what he implies.

"I wanted to help him and I couldn't do that leaving him on the street."

He nods at me, only half amused. I realize his impatience in the way his fingertips tap the table relentlessly. My heart sinks on its own accord. I expected him to be a little more... sympathetic. Friendly. But I shoo the feeling away.

"A lot happened after that. I helped him with his lice. I took him to fly a kite one day. We had grown quite close. But his parents are gone, and he has no family. No siblings, grandparents, cousins... not even a friend. And... I know it is a lot to ask. But..."

I pause and fumble with my purse to get out a pen. Then I grab a napkin, and scribble the street corner onto it. I push it towards him with hot, shaking hands. Goosebumps cover my arms.

"If you could just keep an eye on him. Even if it's only once a week... I know it's a lot to ask... and if I had any other option, I would take it. But you're the only friendly face I know here, and I just want to make sure he's okay. Alive."

I shudder at my own words, and for a short second, Mr. Ghanzali is pushed into my subconscious. And then I hear his voice. But my mind is somewhere else and the words are indistinguishable.

"Sorry?" I ask.

"I said no. I have my own family, Miss… I don't even know your full name. I'm sorry, I just can't."

Sorry? He's sorry? No he isn't. His eyes are steely and his jaw is hard set. This is not up for debate.

"Penelope Whitaker. My name," I whisper. He nods, soundlessly.

All my inhibitions… all my respect for this man dissolves.

"Sorry? You're sorry? I'm not asking you to adopt the kid. Just check on him every once in awhile. It's not such a wild suggestion, so don't treat me as if I have asked you of something so crazy."

I expect Mr. Ghanzali to get angry, to shout at me. Instead, he looks defeated. His shoulders slump and he scrubs at his face, his unkempt beard, until I feel like he's trying to rub his skin off.

"You don't understand," he finally whispers.

"What?"

"You say you know what you are asking of me. But you don't."

"Sir, I-"

"No. Don't say anything. You get to go back to your home in America. You get to go back and forget. Forget about Sooria, about the children, about my- our destroyed homes, our destroyed lives. I had a good life. I had a house. A job. Two daughters. A beautiful wife. And then that bomb hit my house, and everything crumbled with it. What used to be a somewhat solid life, with a few cracks and creaking floors, turned into rubble. Unsalvageable. Gone. Dust. Khalas."

My eyes fall drop and focus on a missing button in his blue shirt.

"So, and I say this with my utmost respect, don't you tell me that you understand. Your life has not been stolen from you, while the media labels you as a potential terrorist. As a hassle, a risk not worth taking because somehow I am a threat to their security. To their people, their children. You don't understand, Miss. And I hope you never do. I would only wish this pain on my worst enemy: on ISIS."

And that is how I am stunned into silence.

His gaze drops and his eyes close, giving me a moment to recollect myself. I force myself to say something, anything. "I- I'm sorry. You're right. I don't understand. I'm sorry I pretended to."

He only nods and my resolve breaks. How can I possibly be angry at him? If roles were reversed, and he had the luxury of being on my side of the table, while I was stuck in his, would I have been able to agree to my request? Would I agree to watch over yet another burden?

I don't think so. But if I am lucky, I will never know. And the roles are not reversed. He is a Syrian refugee with no home, and I am an American citizen who lives in a suburban town with a bachelor's degree at a state university, which my parents paid for. And I give myself all the credit, for working hard. What a joke. I would laugh, but this is too pathetic for me to joke about. So pathetic.

The guilt of Mr. Ghanzali's presence, of his situation and his story, almost leads me out the door with a bowed head and a heavy heart. But then I think about a certain green eyed boy with a heart of gold and a broken will to live. I stay put and I stare Mr. Ghanzali right into his sorrow filled, tired, old eyes, which have seen more than my pretty, microscopic picture of the world could conjure up.

I stare him in the eye, and I know that whatever happens tonight, I have only the world's ignorance to blame.

"I am sorry for what happened to you and your family. But this… this isn't about me. This is about a little boy who has nowhere to go. You said yourself that your life has crumbled. But don't forget, you still have many years on you. Experience. A job. And a family. This boy has nothing except a plastic bag of change and the clothes he wore on his back from Syria."

I plead with him through my voice, my words, my eyes. I plead with him and yet he rejects me. He stands up, without meeting my eye, and he disappears.

Chapter Thirty Two

My shoes come off first. And then my jacket. My arms move robotically, movements only by memory from routine. My hair is wet and frizzed and my clothes are cold and wet. It rained from my walk back from the restaurant. The skies were not full and it was only a drizzle. But the winds were harsh and the walk was long. And now I was freezing and shivering. But this barely registers. I strip and climb into the shower. My hand turns the knob, and I am momentarily shocked by the sudden jets of burning water that hit my skin, my head. And then that too wears off, until my feet keep me upright in the shower. And I am numb once again. I am numb until I feel, really feel the water showering onto me. I literally become washed with the blessing of clean water, and yet, I call myself numb.

I am numb until I am not. Until I wish I was, just so I wouldn't have to feel so much in so little time. I am overwhelmed, flooded with this heart-wrenching, strange pain that I thought I had forgotten. But it hits me all at once, and like this, I remember.

The numbness fades with each play of a certain memory with Ameer. Ameer. Oh God. I think about him and about how he deserves so much more, and how I deserve so much less. What have I done to deserve the flow of water currently spraying onto me. What have I done to deserve a certain blue passport? What have I done to deserve the fortune of being able to cry in a hotel room because life doesn't make sense? And what has Ameer done to deserve only a street corner? Lice? What has he done to deserve being a nameless, friendless, family-less boy in a strange, new city? What is fair about any of this? Mom would be shaking her head in disappointment right now, I think. She always warned me life was unfair. I did not know the extent of this truth. I lost my mother and I thought I understood, more than anyone, what life's cruelty meant. What it felt like.

How wrong I was. How I wish I could be a fool to believe that. But time is arguably the strongest factor in anything. Only time tells. It also takes and gives. My mother got thirty eight years. I am blessed with twenty eight years. Who knows if Ameer will get that much time?

The guilt of wasting water while others die of dehydration catches up with me until I feel compelled to shut off the stream. And then my hands reach for the Dove soap my sister had packed me in her care package, and I feel a velvety, solid material against my skin. I see the soap suds, and I smell a faint, fresh scent. It calms my heightened emotions, and I try to concentrate my focus on getting clean. My mind sways every so often, but I yank it back to covering myself in soap. And then I wash my hair with Pantene shampoo. My eyes sting again, but it might be the tears. I pretend it's the soap.

By the time I am out of the shower, pruned like a raisin and thoroughly washed, I roughly dry myself off with a towel and dry my hair. Habit compels me to brush through the tangles, but I skip brushing my teeth. A small, ridiculous part of me feels guilty for not taking care of myself, but the dominant voice drowns out the other one. I switch the lamp off, double check the doors, and then I climb under the big, white covers. The mattress is soft and springy, but tonight, sleep does not knock. Or maybe I force it away. I'm scared to close my eyes, to become completely out of control of my own head.

I stay like this, squirming and sweaty from anxiety under the covers. It becomes too much for me and I spring up abruptly. I turn on the light and I see the clock through squinted, tired eyes. Eleven o'clock. It feels like time had gone by faster.

I stay like this, still and quiet. But an idle mind is the devil's workshop, and that is never a good thing. So I slouch back onto the cushions and grab my flip phone, and see the missed call.

Syrian Relief Agency.

My heart speeds up and I feel a small moment of euphoria because the anticipation has finally ended. But I also feel sad. Do I really want to go to Syria after everything here? I don't think I could handle it.

My own thoughts remind me of Mr. Ghanzali's words. Hadn't he said something similar to that? He wouldn't help Ameer because he couldn't handle it?

It hurts too much to try to understand him and feel sympathy and sadness, so I replace all this with anger. I replace truth with lies, and then I convince myself that the lie is the truth. Human nature, human ability is a deceptive, dangerous thing.

I can't be like Mr. Ghanzali. So I must accept it. I must. Or else, who am I to judge a man for his limited ability? A hypocrite. And that is the lowest of the low. And those children of Syria… I may be facing a dilemma, but those kids are dying. They need help more than me… more than any of us.

So I breathe through my nose and exhale slowly. And then I call.

Chapter Thirty Three

Three weeks later.

I walk down the metal steps of the aircraft as my arms lug my duffel bag behind me. The air is frigid and still as dark clouds loom over me. They are heavy and full, and they are about to burst. But for now, the air is dry.

I hear sirens in the distance, and people shouting. I see trucks of gasoline and luggage, and buses with passengers driving slowly around the planes. Chaos and a grey smell pollutes the air. My eyes see the beautiful, shimmering lights of Istanbul. But my heart does not tug at the sight like it once did. Things aren't as beautiful anymore; nothing is whimsical. I stand with the other passengers, waiting in solemn quiet. I hear a group of girls laugh and talk amongst themselves, and most others are on their phones, but I just watch. I watch until it is time to board the train. And then I walk onto the bus and stand, my fingertips grazing the cold, metal pole since most seats are taken, and I don't mind standing. The flight was short, but I hate confinement. I frown at the thought of the next flight. It will be much longer, but home is on the other end, and I don't know how I feel about that. The thought of a warm, long shower and a nice bed to myself takes away some of the edge.

My mind is tired, and my heart is sore. My stiff body aches like never before. It reminds me of how I felt after my first ten mile run during cross country practice in freshman year of high school, except this is worse. It isn't only my muscles; my skin still burns from long hours in the snow. Bug bites cover my whole body, and I am riddled with deep cuts from labor. But worse than any of this is my head. It hurts physically to feel or think below surface level. I have felt exhaustion before, but never to this extent. Never to the point where to even think drains me. But I let myself enjoy the fleeting peace from the silence in my own head. It is a rare gift, after all.

This is how I spend the next hour of my life. I pass through customs and security robotically. I collect my baggage without much thought or worry, since all of this seems unimportant. Money is valuable, but only because the world makes it so. There is so much more out there; these past three weeks have taught me this. There are snowball fights, the comfort of warm salted rice in a dirty tent, the energy of family. There is the unparalleled satisfaction of building a school for unfortunate children. Of seeing a mother with tear-filled eyes grasp your hands and thank you. There is the heartbreaking sight of a father on his knees when he discovers his little girl under the rubble. There is an entire village, lost, with only a sack of belongings on their back. There is a grandmother's pain of losing the only home she has ever known, of losing her way of life. There is the smell of smoke and burnt flesh that burns through your nose. There is the stinging of crumbled building scratching your feet. The leathery skin of a child who's been burnt by the sun and stinged by the frost.

I feel the familiar sting in my eyes so I squeeze them shut, until I feel the tears subdue. I have become well

acquainted with the feeling, for the past twenty one nights.
But I try to focus on the weight I roll behind me, on the bite
of the cold air, the smell all cities become. I focus on my plan.
I have a five hour layover, which leaves me with only three
hours to do what I must until I have to get back to the airport.
I let out a long breath through my mouth, which exhales as
a cloud of white smoke. And then I catch a cab with flailing
arms and a shout, and a rusty yellow cab rolls to me abruptly.
The driver rushes out to help me with my luggage, and when I
try to act useful next to him behind the trunk, I catch a strong
whiff of smoke. His teeth are yellow and crooked, and his skin
looks leathery, wrinkled, and burnt. His eyes are sunken deep
into his face, like a creepy doll. His greying hair is cropped
short, and his clothes are stained, smelly, and wrinkled. He is
almost handsome, except there is something unfitting about
the uniform he wears, about the unwillingness to placate me.
He looks like he is meant for so much more than a job as a cab
driver. And yet here he is. Here I am.

I climb in after I halt my staring, but he doesn't seem to
care about my open judgment of him. If he does, he makes no
mention of it. He only opens the back door for me, so I climb
in and he stares at me through his rear view mirror. I tell him
the street name. He frowns at me.

"Hotel name?"

I shake my head, but he is not looking at me anymore.

"No hotel. Just the street."

The rest of the car ride is spent without a word. He
turns on the radio to some Turkish music. I find lyrical music

noisy and hard to appreciate. And yet, the empty sounds that fill my head are surprisingly nice. It drowns out everything else in my head until I am tapping my leg to the beat of the music. The driver taps the wheel and he sings parts of the song, even as he honks and weaves through cars.

I do not count the minutes that pass. The scene blurs in the speed, and I see only fragments of the city. A pole. The train station. A building. The valley as the car swoops down with the curves of the road. My stomach drops at the sudden fall, and the sudden pull of gravity, and then we are up. It reminds me of the takeoff from Syria.

My mind is silent in thought, but pictures, fleeting memories of Syria rush back to me, and I feel myself sinking into an overflow of emotion. I am exhausted from feeling so much. I used to have an off button for all this crap, but that's been gone ever since I got to this place.

I focus on the sight of Ameer. Will he still be in those same clothes, with that plastic bag, begging? Or will he be curled up against the wall, sleeping? I think about his plastic bag of change I found in my purse. I have it with me, even now, in my duffel bag. I imagine walking up to him and giving him the bag. I wonder if he will be happy to see me, or if he will hate me for leaving him so long, without a word. The possibilities are endless.

Finally, the car rolls to a stop at the side of a street where parked cars surround us. The driver turns to me, and I speak the little Turkish that I know to ask him to wait. I would love to stay with Ameer, but reality gets in the way. I have a flight to catch, and I am unwilling to throw away my money to skip this flight and catch one tomorrow. But I have to say goodbye. I have to see him, one last time.

The driver scoffs at me, and then motions for me to calm down. Then he waves me off, and I know he'll wait. I try to smile, but it is wobbly and unfamiliar. So I climb out with my duffel bag, plastic bag clutched in my hand. My feet know the way to that spot, but when I reach, it is empty.

Ameer is gone.

Chapter Thirty Four

Where could he have gone? Where could he be? Where, where, where?

The taxi man honks at me so I walk back to the car frowning, still clutching that plastic bag. I climb into the backseat and sit still, so unsure. Nothing is certain. Nothing is going as I assumed it would.

But life does not abide by the rules. By expectations. It does what it pleases. I have learned this the hard way, and yet, I have forgotten. And without realizing, I do it again.

Surely he will be with Mr. Ghanzali. He must've taken him in. He must've. So I decide to go there. He'll know what happened. I knew he would help Ameer. I just knew it.

I flip through my memories for the name of the restaurant. I come up blank, but I know Mr. Ghanzali. Perhaps this man does too.

"Mr. Ghanzali. You know him? He works at a restaurant?"

The taxi stares at me blankly. Of course. This isn't my four mile hometown, with a whopping population of four thousand. This is Istanbul. I decide on telling him the name of my hotel. The restaurant was walking distance from there. He drives me, muttering under his breath and turning up the radio. I would have frowned at his petulant behavior. But I am too busy worrying, and it is a very soul-sucking, mind numbing job. I worry about missing my flight. I worry about not being able to find the restaurant. But mostly, I worry about Ameer. My heart races, my limbs are jittery, and I sweat like a pig. I tug at the moss green scarf around my neck and swallow hard.

We reach there in a record time of five minutes, but it feels like forever. He halts to a stop, but I point down a street, and he stares at me incredulously, but I am looking down the street. He must see something pretty miserable and pitiful, because the next thing he does is shift gears and drive. My leg is shaking now, but my focus is razor sharp, and finally, I find the building. I tell the driver to stop, and he does, pulling to the side of the street. I ask him with frantic, pleading gestures and broken Turkish and rushed English. This time, he nods at the stuttering idiot that I am and tells me he'll wait in broken, mixed English and Turkish and hand gestures. So I thank him, grab my duffel bag, and I run to the restaurant. I see Mr. Ghanzali talking to a couple in Turkish, motioning for them to go to the restaurant. He smiles at them like the great advertiser he is. That is, until he sees me. And then he smiles at them impatiently, and leads them to the restaurant. But they refuse, and continue their walk. I walk up to him.

"Ms. Penelope, I did not expect you. How are you?"

"Good. Where is he?"

He stares at me pitifully. "Who?"

But he knows exactly who. He is procrastinating. I refuse to imagine why.

I am about to lose it, and I think he knows this, because he leads me down into the alley.

"Why don't we go talk in the restaurant? You can get something to eat, or drink if you're not hungry. Or we could-"

"Mr. Ghanzali."

He stops his rambling, and looks anywhere but at me.

"Where is he?"

"Who?" he mumbles.

"Ameer. The boy I told you about. Did you ever see him?"

"I told you I couldn't."

"That's not an answer."

I force him to look me in the eye. He looks more nervous than I feel.

"Yes. I went, once."

My heart beats so frantically. Until it stills.

"And? How is he? I went to see him before my flight back home. But he wasn't there. Is he with you?"

"No."

I grow impatient and angry. I used to like treasure

hunts, but this cryptic talk is getting on my nerves.

"Then what? What aren't you telling me?"

He stares at me with pity. I don't like it. And then he speaks. "He's gone, Miss."

My anger evaporates. It is replaced with worry. I think I'm going to have a panic attack. But I have to know. I think he can see it too, as I sway on my feet. His eyes swarm with concern. "Maybe we should go inside. You should sit--"

"Gone how?"

"I really think we should--"

"Tell m-?"

"He's dead."

Chapter Thirty Five

I hear my breath whoosh out of me before I feel it. My knees tremble and I'm dizzy. I think I might faint. My hands shake and I struggle to squeeze them into fists. But once I do, my nails bite my skin until they tear its surface, until it is stinging. I keep grasping.

"How?" I hear myself croak.

"The temperature dropped a few days ago. There was no snow, but there was sleet before the temperature dropped. I checked for him the next morning, but... but I was too late. He was... slumped on the street. His clothes were soaking. People were already crowded around him. I... I got him a burial. There was no headstone. I would have but I couldn't afford it. But I got him a plot for a grave. He got to be buried. But I didn't save him. I was too late."

My world freezes and I stand there like the stupid fool I am. I say nothing. I feel hot tears run down my cold cheeks, leaving a trail of wetness. They dribble down my neck and then my shirt, finally getting caught in the tight fabric. I try to stop them from instinct, but eventually, I quit. They run freely until my shoulders shake and my eyes hurt and my heart feels heavy and weighed down by the burden of guilt, of pain. Of loss.

The world should not be turning like it is. This dirty, corrupt place did not deserve someone like Ameer. But now he's gone, and it's like nothing changed. The air is still charged, and the world continues to spin.

The world continues to spin.

I wipe at the now cold tears, until my hands and sleeves are wet with them. Mr. Ghanzali offers me a napkin as he looks at me with guilt and pity. I don't accept it. Instead, I turn around and leave him. But he shouts after me, and I am too weak to stop him when he takes me by the shoulders and leads me back to the alley. I feel hot tears stream down my face, but he makes no mention of them.

"I'm sorry, Miss. Truly. But you go home, okay? Go home and kiss your family. Sleep in your bed and count your blessings. Don't forget about your boy. Don't let it take you over. Don't quit. Be strong. But, when you feel like you can, do something about it. You have so much. And if you wanted, if you really tried, you could save a lot of Syria."

There is so much I want to say, so much I want to shout. But I only nod and cry some more. I don't trust myself to speak. Or maybe I can't.

"Take care, Miss. Take care."

And then I say goodbye, because some fragmented, reasonable part of me knows I will regret it later if I don't.

"You too. Good luck with your family. And... thank you."

I'm not sure what I thank him for. But somehow, I feel gratitude for him. For his brief presence in my life. He nods in response. And then his eyes widen.

"I almost forgot. I have something of Ameer's. I... just wait here, please. I'll go get it." And then he sprints to the restaurant. I think about leaving him, and going back to the taxi. I can hear honking, and I see the cab drive slowly until he stops right where I am. He looks angry. But he must see something on my face. I see him huff, but he parks the car.

Mr. Ghanzali runs back to me, this time with a grocery bag. Something painfully familiar pokes out of it. The kite. He hands me the bag.

"I saw a plastic bag filled with this stuff. I figured if there was one person to give this to, it was you. It has some clothes, a kite, and the coins he collected."

"Thank you."

I look inside the bag. "Thank you," I repeat.

He nods at me. "Good luck with everything, Ms. Penelope."

"You too, Mr. Ghanzali. I wish you the best."

We nod at each other, and he smiles at me warmly. I try to replicate it, only partially succeeding. And then I am walking away from him and towards the taxi. Away from this, and back home. God knows I need it right now. And with that, I say goodbye to Istanbul. I try to do the same to a certain green-eyed boy.

I fail miserably.

Chapter Thirty Six

Ever since I signed up for the Syrian Aid trip, I thought about what it would be like when I returned home. Would I be thrilled to see Dad and Abby? Would I have a big party for my return? Would my friends pick me up? Or would I miss Istanbul and Syria so much that I would hate coming back? My even bigger mistake was making expectations. I tried not to; I really did. But they couldn't be helped. I had a million possibilities all conjured up to detailed perfection, and I always expected things to turn out as I imagined they would, but they seldom did.

This time was no exception. I never imagined I would be mourning the loss of a friend on my way back home. I never imagined I would feel this much pain as I returned from a trip that I hoped would be good for me. Eye opening.

This just felt toxic.

I sit next to the window, and there is an old Arab man snoring next to me. He smells like grease and fried food and sweat, but I don't mind it. Something about him is familiar, and he reminds me of Ameer. While he does not have that youthful innocence, he has an overflowing awkward kindness about him. And there is that... feeling about him. He's lost something so great that the rest of us could only pretend to understand. And yet there is this dim, minute of hope in his eyes. In the way he smiles at me when I greet him, and in the way his tense shoulders set back in a fierce determination.

I close my eyes as the plane jerks in tribulation. I had found some artist that sounded familiar- Adele, I think- and I played her album. Now, in a desperate attempt to find some silence in my loud mind, I turn up the volume and set my shoulders back, but the lyrics don't do the trick. They fill the space until that too fades into the background, and I am left thinking about everything I want so badly to forget. I rip off the black headphones and toss them to the ground. I squirm in my seat. I am already tense; this crowded, dry air isn't help-ing. My mom used to tell me to journal whenever I felt like this. She did it all the time, whenever she felt overwhelmed. I always waved off the suggestion. My shrinks suggested it too. I was forced to keep a journal, and I wrote in it once. It did nothing but bring back all the pain, so I learned to suppress everything, and I became an expert at it. And then I lost that ability in Istanbul, and I am left drowning in all of this. So I pull out that hotel notepad and pen I always swipe whenev-er I go to a hotel. I click the pen on, and then let it caress the paper. I don't know what to write, so I start with the date.

March 17, 2016
And then I begin.

Chapter Thirty Seven

I expect myself to write a journal entry, but it ends up being a letter to Ameer. The words are broken and jumbled, but they convey what I want them to, and even as I reread the letter for the fourth time and I discover every flaw with every sentence, there is something beautiful about the messy, imperfection of it all. And it feels good. When I start the letter, I feel like a badly scarring wound is getting slashed open. But when I end it, I feel an inexplicably brief moment of total calm. And then the chaos is back. But there is a subconscious part of me that knows things will get better.

I'm sorry I didn't stay. I'm sorry I didn't save you.

Maybe I'm a masochist, because I read these lines over and over again, until I have memorized the words. Until it replays in my head like a broken record. Until I feel the familiar sting in my eyes, followed by the spilling of wetness onto my face and down my neck. I stop my breaths so that I don't embarrass myself any further and start wailing and sobbing. I roughly wipe away the tears, rubbing at my skin so harshly that it stings. And then I rub my eyes, and shake my head. My eyes sting again, but I squeeze them so hard that they subdue. I feel the familiar throb in my head, and I rub at my temples.

Ameer,

My God, I miss you. I didn't expect things to end like this. I didn't expect you to be gone so soon. If there was anything I could do to bring you back, I would. But you're gone and nothing is going to change that.

I think if you were here, you'd be very disappointed in me. I left those kids in Syria, Ameer. I left them. It hurt me too much to see them every day. I left so much of myself there. And believe me when I say that I really wanted to stay. But I left a week early. Isn't that so pathetic?

I couldn't even save you. I tried, Ameer. I did. I went to this man I knew, Mr. Ghanzali. I went and asked him to take care of you. But he was too late. You were already dead when he got there. He kept going on and on about giving you a burial. But what do I care about a burial? You deserve so much more than a plot of dirt, six feet under.

I'm sorry I didn't stay. I'm sorry I didn't save you. I love you, kid. I think I loved you the moment I saw you curled up against that wall. And maybe we'll meet again, in another life. But for now, I'll just settle for a letter you'll never read. What else can I do?

Penelope

Chapter Thirty Eight

Sleep escapes me. I have only brief moments of such exhaustion that I close my eyes and reach the brink of unconsciousness. But the tightness of space and the stale air and my thoughts catch up with me every time and stop me from sleeping. By the time we land, my eyes are so heavy, harsh sunlight makes them ache . I push open the window as the pilot warns the plane for landing. I think it is strangely beautiful that I saw that same sun in Syria and in Istanbul. No matter where I am in the world, I can always count on seeing the same sky.

When the seatbelt light turns off, I take off the belt and collect my bag. I double check the seat pockets as my mother always forced us to do. And then I stand on my stiff legs and numb feet. My heart beats a little faster at finally getting out of this confining space, at the thought of sunshine and fresh air and home. I feel the warmth and comfort of home. Because no matter how dysfunctional family is, no matter how awful school or work is, home is where the heart is. I know this from experience, and days after a long period of loneliness. Days like today.

Finally I am off the plane and climbing down yet another metal staircase. I greedily breathe in the air of California, and I grin for the first time in forever. Home.

I feel re-energized despite the serious lack of sleep and drop from caffeine that I am currently experiencing. I can't wait to get my hands on a good cup of Starbucks. That's one thing I won't miss about Istanbul their coffee.

I can't wait for my warm bed, my own apartment, and my peanut butter. Also, in a strange way, I am excited to see my family. I love them even when they act like complete nut heads. It's part of my genetic makeup.

I look around me when I am finally on the bus, and for a moment, I am stumped. Everyone is speaking English. I am surrounded by white people. Jeans, t-shirts. I blend right in, which feels odd after my weeks spent surrounded by Turkish people and Muslims and unfamiliarity.

In a strange way, I like feeling like I blend in. I feel accepted. No one has a problem with a white girl who has green eyes and brown hair and pale skin.

I take out my iPhone and turn off airplane mode. My phone buzzes a million times and I see a flood of notifications. One in particular catches my eye. A cluster of texts from Dad and Abby. I flick through them. The last one lets me know that they're running late. I feel a little disappointed and irritated, but I force it away, because I know it's just a load of sleep deprivation and homesickness. But mostly sleep deprivation. My phone tells me it is just after two. I yawn and my eyes droop, but they swing back open when the bus lurches to a stop, and my empty, butterfly-filled stomach lurches with it. I feel a bit like puking, but that hasn't happened since last year when I ate two burritos from Taco Bell.

I climb off the bus and the next hour consists of long lines, security checks, immigration officers, and finally, baggage claim. When I have my purple suitcase and duffel bag adorned with stickers with me, I text Dad. He tells me he's waiting in front of the terminal. My throbbing eyes squint and scan the queue of cars. I spot the sparkling silver BMW. My heartbeat increases as I fumble with my luggage and rush to the car, and I take a deep breath and push open the airport door. I breathe in the frosty, polluted air. Home.

He sees me and gets out of the car, grinning. He walks to me and I leave the suitcase for a second and wrap my arms around him. He's wearing designer khakis and an embarrassing cartoon character shirt, with the character he invented, but I've gotten used to it by now. He still smells like rich cologne (Dad hates Axe), and he's wearing his favorite Armani shades. We pull apart as my arms get sore from reaching up to wrap around him. Dad grins and I almost effortlessly get myself to smile back.

"I missed you, kid."

"Missed you too, Dad." And I mean it. Even if he does dress like a snobbish rich middle school boy. And if he's never really there when he should be. He's here now and that's what matters. That's what has to matter.

He pops open the truck and I let him put my suitcases in after an insincere offer to help him. He shakes his head and laughs when I shrug my shoulders and climb into the car. I close my eyes and feel the exhaustion of the plane and lack of sleep catch up to me. I hear the trunk close, and the door open. I open my eyes and look at Dad as he put the car into drive. Zayn Malik blasts from the speakers and Dad lowers the volume. I smirk.

"What are you smiling at?" he asks.

"I always suspected you had a man crush on Zayn. It's only confirmed now." I don't try to stop the wave of laughter. I haven't heard it in a while, and it feels good. Fleeting, but good.

The tips of Dad's ears turn crimson. "It was the only decent song playing."

I laugh some more until Dad awkwardly changes the

subject.

"So how was the trip?"

My laughter dims. "Good. It was good. I really enjoyed it," I fumble.

Dad shoots me a look. "You're back a week early." He says this carefully, as if he is treading dangerous waters. I don't like it. Even if these are dangerous waters.

"It was pretty exhausting. Emotionally and physically... I don't regret going but I think it was good to come back early," I tell him. Lies only lead to more lies, and I've always preferred the truth. And it works. The tension and fragility of the conversation lessons.

"Well... it's nice to have you back."

"It's nice to be back."

Let's see how long that lasts.

Chapter Thirty Nine

Dad asks me if I want to stop by my apartment first, but I turn the offer down. Maybe I'm a masochist, or stupidly hopeful in this whole family thing, but I want home. Dad smiles when I say this, and he turns down the radio.

"So, listen."

Uh oh. No good ever comes out of a conversation that starts off like that. I tense in my seat, but Dad continues.

"Abby got a huge client last week, so she's at this meeting for it right now. But we're going to have dinner tonight. As a family, the three of us. I want you to play nice. We've missed you these past few weeks, both of us. Tonight, I just want to have a good family reunion. Okay?"

Okay? No, there's nothing okay about this. That's what I want to say, but my filter blocks the words. So I nod and stay silent. Dad turns up the radio after that to block out the awkward silence.

I look out the window and feel a strange sense of remembrance and forgetting. The scenery comes back to me as a long lost familiarity. There is something comfortingly familiar and oddly new about home. Nothing has changed, and yet everything feels different. There are no rolling hills, fruit stands, swarms of pedestrians, yelling market men, refugees swarming the streets… no Ameer.

I squeeze my eyes shut so tightly that when I open them, the sunlight suddenly becomes very prominent. That is one thing that is the same, wherever I go. I find peace knowing that this is the same sun I saw on the other side of the world, only a couple days ago.

And then Dad turns onto the street. Our street. We drive past long lines of evergreens and trimmed bushes and planted flowers that are only beginning to bloom. We drive past artificially colored endless land of vibrant green lawns. I see the sprinklers and ostentatious decorations, like fountains, elaborate sculptures, and uniquely trimmed bushes. And then we drive up to our house, and for a moment, I am floundered by it. Is it really this big? This extravagant? This beautiful? I think back to the refugee camps in Syria, made of miles of tents and dirt and snow. Miles of stranded children, of families. Our house could fit at least 100 of those people.

I ignore this thought, because what else can I do? Dad pulls onto the driveway and shuts off the car. I climb out, stretching and breathing deeply. The air is wet, chilled, and breezy, and it wakes me from my sleepy state. Then I see it. A huge, obnoxious Trump and Pence sign sits on the lawn.

I look away from the poster, and I turn to Dad. He sets my suitcase on the ground, puffing out white air. He looks up at me, and I'm still gaping like a fish. He must realize what I'm so shocked about, because he points to the sign and grins. It looks so similar to the monster in the poster that a shiver runs down my back, and it's not from March weather.

"D'you like it? It came last week. I thought it might surprise you."

"Do... do I like it? What do you think?" I sound like nails on a chalkboard, and we both cringe. But then my dad looks up at me, confused.
"So... you like it?"

"Is this a joke? Are you trying to be funny? What, April Fools or something? Because this isn't funny. It's immature. Right, of course. It's a joke. It has to be," I am out of breath by the time I'm done, but I don't know if it's from the odd rambling or the oncoming panic attack. I'm going to be an optimist and say the first one.

"April Fools? No, honey. Although, I did have this awesome prank this year. I think it might have even beaten the water balloons. But, anyway. That's not the point. Do you not like the guy?"

I take a deep breath so that I don't combust, right here, on the driveway. Although I'm not sure why I try to keep it in. Maybe it would do my dad some good to get some sense kicked into him.

"No, Dad. I do not like him. No sane person does. Especially no self-respecting woman."

He laughs awkwardly. "Woah, exaggeration much? Why are you so worked up, anyway? I never thought you were so passionate about politics."

"This isn't about politics, Dad!"

"Honey, the guy's running for president. I'd say that's pretty political. But, whatever. We can talk about this later. You're tired and crank-- I mean, tired. And… and let's just go in, okay? I have a new cartoon I want to show you!"

He practically pushes me into the house, while awkwardly balancing a suitcase and my duffel bag with his left hand. I'm still boiling when we get inside, but I see the welcome home banner, and try to forget about the anger. But I can't forget about it. It simmers down when I see my dad's boyish smile, and I force myself to smile back. He's still my dad, even if he is a racist, sexist, Donald fan. He's still my dad. Some things don't change.

Chapter Forty

After a tense hug, and one episode of Parks and Rec I force myself to watch with Dad, I make up an excuse and slug my way upstairs to my old room. I haven't redecorated since freshman year of high school, so, as I always do when I enter, I half cringe and half smile. The bed is twin sized and there are fairy tale like purple drapes on three sides. The desk is stark white and scratched, with a black rolling chair I spent a lot of time on. The walls are relatively bare, with only a few photo frames of my friends and I, light-years ago. Dad bought me this massive abstract painting for one wall. I think the plainness of my room bothered him, considering art is his profession and his life, but I never cared. The room was quiet, solitary, and clean. Neat. I didn't need anything else.

I crawl under the cool covers in my dark, shadowed room and my eyes close. I toss my phone and hear it land with a thud, then I fumble with my shoes until those get kicked off too. The jacket stays on, after a lazy struggle to get it off. And that is how I fall asleep. Still simmering, sad, and undone. Because I might be in my teenage room, but for some reason, I miss home. My heart aches in longing for it, and then in despair because I'm pretty sure I'll never get it.

But I have a bed, a house, and a family. And a serious case of sleep deprivation. So I fall asleep anyway. But when I wake up three hours later, I am completely drained.

My eyes close and suddenly, I am back in Turkey, walking up to Ameer. His eyes are closed, so my fingertips skim his shoulders to wake him up. But he's too cold. Too still. So I press my hand to his neck, to check for a heartbeat. There isn't one. I shake his shoulders, as if this will bring him back, and it does. He opens his eyes, but the greens and golds are gone, replaced with an aching, empty grey. He cries into my palms and he asks me why I left him. I don't know what I say, but it doesn't matter. His eyes close and he is still again.

And then I am in a tent. I am shivering and puffs of stark white come from my mouth. My teeth chatter and my throat aches. I crawl to a faceless baby and touch his shoulders. But he whimpers and tears escape him. He's shivering and his skin prickles with goosebumps. I touch his cheeks and they are ice. I take off my jacket and the bitter cold bites at me now. But then I wake up and I don't think about this and cover the baby with my jacket, but it's not enough. He stays warm for a while, until it is night and the temperature drops. His heartbeat vanishes. The baby stills.

And then I am in my apartment. I hear my laughter, and the sound of someone familiar. I am stirring something in the kitchen, and I feel arms encircle me until they begin tickling me. I turn around and I see Ameer. I feel warm and light. He's there, with me, in blue jeans and a basketball team jersey. I am yelling at him to put a jacket on, but I know I'm still smiling. I reach over to grab him and pull him in towards me. But there is nothing but air. I look at my hands confused, and then I look up. Ameer is gone. And I am screaming.

I yank off the covers and stand. I pant like I've just run a marathon and my heart races. I press my hand to it, and feel it thumping in my chest. I close my eyes and that is all I can feel. My own heartbeat. A tear slips. I'm still here. I'm still here.

I think about the dream, and another tear escapes me. His heart has long since stopped. While my hands are clammy with sweat, his are cold as ice. While I am two stories high living the American dream, he is six feet under, dead.

I sway in my semi-consciousness and slide to the floor. My head falls back until I am lying down, knees up. My eyes close and a few more tears escape. I almost feel peace. And then I hear padded footsteps and Abby yelling for me. My eyes shoot open, and I scrub at my face and get up in frantic, jerking movements. I open the door and Abby leaps at me like a monkey, curling legs and all. My heart races at the sudden intrusion, but I try to return to normalcy. I see my arms wrap around her and I hear my throaty, awkward laugh. She hops off me, and thank God for that since I'm already unsteady on my wobbling legs. She grabs my faces and squeezes my cheeks until my lips are pressed together like a fish. She stares at me, laughter quieting.

"Are you okay? You look like you've been crying," she blurts.

I yawn, making it more dramatic than it is. "Oh, yeah. I'm fine. I was just sleeping."

She pinches at my cheek and I stare at her as if to question her sanity.

"Eyelash."

I nod. The silence is awkward, but with Abby in the room, it doesn't last long. I think I might hate her for that. I always make things awkward; she eradicates it.

She pushes me to sit on my unmade bed, and then pulls open the curtains. Sunlight showers the room, and things don't seem so dark anymore. I feel my spirits lift. And then she opens her mouth.

"So, how was your trip?" she tries to sound casual, but she's surprisingly bad at pretending.

"Good. Great. It was great."

"That's… good. I'm glad your back, though. We were pretty worried, you know. You didn't exactly go to the safest place in the world."

I try not to snort. "Well, no need to worry. I'm all good."

She frowns. "No need to worry? There was plenty of reason to worry. Do you watch the news?"

I sigh. She's right about this. There is plenty reason to worry. "You're right. I'm sorry. I think I'm just super tired. Sleeping on an airplane is pretty impossible," I say, trying to move onto another subject. I don't feel like arguing anymore today.

"That's funny, since you used to go out like a light whenever we flew to California in the summer." I hate the way she says it. As if I have personally offended her by keeping a huge secret.

But I take a deep breath because I know I'm overreacting. Or maybe not. But none of that matters. Today is turning out very differently than how I imagined it would, and I don't like it. So I've given up on arguing, at least for now. Today, I will swallow what I really want to say.

"Dad said you got a new client."

"What? Oh, yes. Last week. It's a baby shower! I'm so excited. I mean, Sherry, the mom, she wants a green theme. Apparently it's the new pink. But I think it's a little… dumb. Pink would've been so much cuter. Oh well. I guess I'll just have to wait for your baby to come!"

I snort. "Right. Why don't you wish for world peace? I'm sure that'll come around sooner."

"Miss Congeniality reference?"

"I don't know what you're talking about."

"Oh, come on! You loved that movie when you were in high school!"

"Yeah, well, in case you haven't noticed… I'm not in high school anymore."

She looks around the room and her nose twitches. I roll my eyes at her drama. "This room says differently. And whatever, I don't care how old you are. You'll always be in love with that movie."

"Fine, you caught me. I just wish the sequel was better."

"Yeah right! Pirates, Miss Universe, a bank robbery… it's so random!"

I laugh and she joins in. We fall onto the bed like hyenas and giggle like teenage girls. It feels good. I forget about Trump, Ameer, and the storm that's brewing out of my little California bubble. I get to forget, and for that, I am grateful.

Chapter Forty One

Dad makes a seafood dinner. Jumbo shrimp (which seems like an oxymoron to me), marinated lobster, filleted salmon, and brown rice. We sit around the massive, oak dining table with the chandelier illuminating the room. Everything looks magical under it, and I can almost pretend like this is normalcy.

"I still remember how much you loved going to Red Lobster. We went there for your seventh birthday, remember? 'Cause I do," Dad boasts like a little kid showing off his drawing to his parents.

I know he wants me to feel touched, and to feel like his daughter again. And when I look at his obvious effort, I almost do, but even this is a lie. I never liked seafood as a kid. But Mom loved it and I wanted to feel like we had something in common. And it worked perfectly, well, other than the fact that I was lying. But it became our thing. On those rare Mommy-me moments, we spent it on seafood. And we went to Red Lobster's for my tenth birthday and it ended in a disaster. But I don't tell him this. I'll placate him tonight. And probably the night after this, and the one after that. Because that's what I do and some things can't change, no matter how much I want them to. Some things are better off as they are.

So I nod and smile and placate. "Yeah, I remember. Thank you, Dad. I love everything. It's perfect."

He grins back. Abby smiles smugly, as if she planned this all along. As if the family, or what's left of it, is finally functioning. I would laugh if this wasn't so sad.

The lobster is overcooked and over salted, but I eat it anyway. And then I reprimand myself for complaining about it. It wouldn't matter if I was eating squid and goat brain. At least I'm not living in pile of rubble, starving. Dying. Yes.

Thank God I'm not there.

Dinner continues in awkward, forced phases. Or maybe it's just me. Abby and Dad seem to be having a grand time. They're laughing about something, and I smile along. But I'm not hearing anything. That is, until I hear my name in their conversation.

"...And Nellie over here freaked on me when she saw the sign I got for the lawn. I forgot how cranky she gets when she's tired. I bet she didn't sleep much over... there."

Abby's smile never breaks, but something dims in her eyes. Maybe it's at the mention of "there," but I know it isn't. But I don't spend much time analyzing her reaction, because I'm a little occupied trying not to blow up in front of my dad here. I don't know how to go about decoding all those hidden (and not-so-hidden) insults he just threw at me. For a man depleted in the communications department, he sure knows how to pack a punch in two sentences. And the sad part is, I don't think he even realizes how mean he can be.

Maybe if my dad wasn't a racist, ignorant-

I stop the insult in my head before it can complete. Part of me is too scared to speak, to think. I don't want this night to get any worse than it already has. But the dominant voice in my head is pissed. But when I'm this mad, I turn frozen. My brain freezes over, my throat closes, and the anger never lasts. It fades into despair, into self-pity, and loathing, until all I want to do is crawl back into bed and have a good cry.

The switch to my emotions is back. I turn them off.

Chapter Forty Two

Dinner ends and we move to the island in the kitchen for dessert. Abby made coffee flavored macaroons, triple chocolate brownies, and vanilla cupcakes with caramel frosting.

"Here's my special hot chocolate," Abby grins and hands me a hot pink mug that is topped with whipped cream and mini marshmallows. I smile and thank her, but inside I'm rolling my eyes. What's so special about it? She uses skimmed milk (yuck), expensive bitter chocolate (really bitter), and then balances it out with loads of honey to be healthy. Hmm. I believe unique is a more fitting description. I drink it tentatively, and try not to choke. I bite into what really is my favorite: the brownies. They're overly sweet and artificially flavored and pure perfection. Abby's nose crinkles when she sees me moaning over them.

"I would've made them homemade, but I know you like the boxed ones better. God knows why," she mumbles.

I grin, for real this time. "I find joy in the little things."

"Yeah. The little things that'll kill you before you're forty," she tells me. I just laugh. It's a nasty, snorting, obnoxiously loud laugh, but nothing can stop me. Well, except for a handful of brownie getting shoved into my mouth. Abby's frowning and smiling at me simultaneously. I grin at her with a mouthful of brownie. God, what's causing this?

"You're disgusting. And in a couple years, you're going to be disgusting and fat."

"More of me to love!"

"Since when are you such a sap? And a weirdo?"

"Hey, I've always been weird on the inside. And you bring out the cheesiness in me. Maybe I'm just happy to see you."

This time, Abby is the one to snort. It's a small, ladylike one, and she goes red the minute it's out. Dad enters the room with his hands behind his back and a grin that scares me. There have been a lot of those ever since I got home. I used to think I was being pessimistic, but if I'm always right, then isn't it just realism? This thought makes me sad, so I ignore it, and quite easily too. It gets pushed to the very back of my mind, until it is a little blip in the distance. I'm happy to leave it there.

Dad walks up to me and brings forward his surprise. I expect it to be a canvas, but it's a velvet jewelry box the color of sunshine. My mouth parts and I take the box from him. Next to me, a grinning, glowing Abbie speaks.

"I helped choose the design," she blurts. Dad rolls his eyes at her and she glares back. But they're both grinning. I feel a pang of jealousy, and then an overwhelming swarm of guilt. They're giving me a present they're obviously proud of. I should be thankful.

The box is a long rectangle, and I expect a silver

necklace inside. But it is so much more. The box is harder to open, but it snaps after a few tries, and I am shocked by what I see. A delicate gold chain holds a charm that I know Dad made. I can tell by the little imperfections, the personal touches. It is made of black marble, and it has been carved into the shape of a sun. I've never liked gold, but it is hard not to find the unique beauty of this. I stare at the intricate detail on the sun. There are patterns made of paisleys, swirls and dots on one side. On the other side, a message of carved in and painted gold. "Home." And then there is a set of numbers underneath it. I look up in part confusion, part wonder. Dad grins back. "The coordinates of the house. Of home."

With the necklace in one hand and the box in another, I wrap my arms around Dad and squeeze until it is death grip. He lets out a gasp and awkward chuckle but his arms wound around me. Lightly at first, and then he is squeezing me back, and then his arms go limp again. But I don't let go. I feel Abby's skinny arms wrap around me and Dad from the back, and she buries her head in my hair on my right shoulder and inhales deeply. We stay like this for a finite infinity. The moment ends, but I'll never forget this.

Family is all we have. And I'll take mine as they are. Even if we have a Trump sign in our front lawn. Even if they'll never understand the world Ameer lived in.

Yes. Even then.

Chapter Forty Three

I drive to my own apartment the morning after. I wave goodbye to Dad as I try to ignore the glaring, ugly sign in the lawn. And then I drive away, breathing out a sigh of relief, and then another of longing. Is it possible for a person to miss someone and be glad to be rid of them, all at once? Because that's how I feel right now. I feel the cool marble sun on my chest, and I feel peace and chaos all at once. It's too much. I turn it off.

I stop for coffee at Starbucks on the way home. I'm not even sure I want it, but it feels like a habit that I can't break because of the comforting regularity of it. I don't like change. I turn into my neighborhood and I feel a sense of calm upon me. This may not be home, but it is familiar. And I can always find peace in that. I park in front of my apartment and get out of the car. The luggage is a challenge, since I only have my own pair of hands, but I manage. I walk up a flight of old metal stairs and unlock the door. The apartment has two floors and I get the top one. My neighbors downstairs are rather odd- an eccentric couple who love to fight at random times of the night- but they generally keep to themselves and I don't mind the expected annoyance. Another thing I can rely on.

My apartment is exactly as I left it. In a complete disarray, but clean. The kitchen is on the left and the living space is on the right. Further down, my room and en suite bathroom are behind the kitchen, while a cramped, dusty study is across from it on the left. The apartment is old and the appliances are unreliable, but it is clean. Simple. Minimalistic. The floor is sandalwood brown, except for a warm, burgundy rug in the living room. The kitchen is cramped and there is little counter space, which is entirely made of worn brown laminate, while the cabinets are a dusty sand color, similar to the floors in the rest of the place. The kitchen floor is entirely brown tile. Brown floor, brown cabinets, brown counters… the only other color in the kitchen comes from coffee mugs that hang next to the whiteish refrigerator, and my colorful cutting boards (a gift from Abby).

On the left, there are two cream colored couches, bought used from Ebay, and there is a dark brown coffee table in the middle, with two matching round ones next to each of the couches. There is a small, cheap flat screen Dad forced me to accept. I hated taking it, but with each episode of Parks and Rec (and occasionally Property Brothers), I became more attached to it. The TV sits on a teetering table that is the color of ash and has been through more wear-and-tear that my childhood teddy, Morby. Even I cringe a little every time my eyes zone in on it, but it's better than nothing.

An abstract of reds, blues, yellows, greens, oranges, and every other color except white and black and brown hangs between two teeny windows, complete opposite of the kitchen. Dad got it for me and hung it up himself (well, tried to). It's a little lopsided, but it's my most and least favorite part of my apartment. Even to my untrained eyes, it is clear to me that this piece of art is beautiful and exactly what I need in an apartment. But I think I hate it because Dad gave it to me.

I close my eyes and hold in a breath. My chest feels

tight, as it has for days, and I don't know how to get rid of the pressure. I feel brand new and completely old. And I'm tired. It's the kind of exhaustion that cannot be cured by sleep or suppressed by caffeine. But I don't know what can cure it, so I leave my suitcase at the front door, kick off my sneakers, sling my jacket on the black coat rack, and walk to the bedroom. Then I push open the sandalwood door, and I fall into my lavender cotton sheets. Sleep isn't a cure but it comes to me anyway. And I take it, because I don't know what else to do.

And I'm not ready for life to change. Even if it does suck in some ways.

Chapter Forty Four

Monday morning comes faster than I expect, but I don't mind it. In fact, I strangely look forward to it. It's exhausting, mentally and emotionally, but it is rewarding in equal amounts. As a registered nurse for a nursing home, I don't usually make an effort to look good. But this morning is different. Or maybe I'm just desperate for some sort of change, no matter how much it scares me. I'm trying, and my effort comes in the form of French braided hair, foundation, mascara, and nude lipstick.

I wear my usual white scrubs and matching shoes, and my worn black bag. I even wake up half an hour early so I can make breakfast. I plan for an omelet and toast, but it ends up being scrambled eggs, an apple, and coffee. I try not to let it dampen my determination to enjoy the day, but it works only partially.

I drive my silver Camry to work, which is a twenty minute drive. I get there ten minutes early and a certain sense of belonging is bestowed upon me when my coworkers and acquaintances wave at me as I park and get out of the car. I smile and they greet me with loose hugs and grins.

Margaret loops my arm through her and I let her, awkwardly. She's a petite, kind girl with brown doe eyes and hair the color of flames that is cropped to her head. I don't like the color or the length, but I don't tell her this.

"You changed your hair. Looks good!"

She rolls her eyes and laughs this laugh that bothers me quite a bit. "Oh, this old thing? Yeah, I figured it was time for a change," she says with a casual smile, cool as a cucumber. Oddly, it reminds me of Myrtle in The Great Gatsby. They both act like they don't care the slightest about what people think of them, but I know the truth. Compliments and acceptance is what they live for.

Sharon lags behind us, tapping away with long manicured fingers on her phone. She wears the same uniform as the rest of us, but her dangling earrings, African style braids, and perfect makeup gives her a unique style, even in plain scrubs. I envy her cool attitude, because she honestly doesn't care what I- or anyone else- thinks. I may mock Margaret for her desperation, but aren't I the same way? From Dad, from my friends… from Mom. I act like none of it matters, but it does. I just gave up after years of failing to be the center of anyone's attention.

But my thoughts are silenced when Margaret pushes through the glass doors and into the nursing home, dragging me with her. The air is stale, and it smells like old people and disinfectant. The potted plants are cheap and fake, and the lighting is dim and sad. The brown furniture and brown carpet is dated and dull. But oh, am I glad to be back. I feel myself simultaneously forget and remember what this normal, habitual routine feels like. My feet know where to go, my hands know where to sign on the chart, and a built in sense in my head knows that I am somewhere familiar.

Someone familiar, Toby, I think, tells me with disinterest and a slight twinge of unwarranted bitterness, that Gabriella wants to see me. My heart speeds up at the mention of my boss, but only because I miss her. She's one of the few who work here that I look forward to seeing.

I go down the familiar hall of white walls and brown… everything, until I reach the last, sand colored door. I take a deep breath, because she is still my boss, and knock with a slight hesitance. I hear a muffled response, and I open the door and enter. Gabriela sits at her desk on the left, staring at her computer. The light from it glares onto her thickly rimmed, oval shaped grey glasses. She has the frizziest and blackest hair I've ever seen. There is not a speck of grey, despite her age, which I suspect is somewhere in the forties or fifties. She wears her signature black blazer and matching pants, with a cactus green shirt. Her hair is unfettered today, and it frames her face loosely like a halo. Her nutmeg skin is flawless and she wears only her signature matte maroon lip-stick.

She looks up and her dark as night eyes catch my glossy green ones. She leaps from her black chair and the next thing I know, her arms wrap around me like a vice. I squeeze back and my heart warms at her overwhelming warmth, because it is rare I get to feel this way. She releases me and grips my shoulders. Her laughing eyes look straight into my struggling ones, and she gives me one of her rare, motherly smiles. Like she knows something about me that I don't. I saw it when she first offered me a job as an RN and I refused blatantly. I saw it when I told her I was quitting after a patient and my good friend, Molly Sniders, died. And I see it now.

As I always do in nerve-racking situations, I laugh awkwardly and my mind blanks. Her eyes laugh at me and she presses her lips together to stop a teeth-baring, childish grin. But she senses my uncomfortableness as I squirm, and she breaks her gaze and leads me to the two grey chairs that are opposite from hers. But she sits in the chair close to me and grips my hands. Gabriela expresses her affection physically, but I don't mind it.

"So, how was the trip? How was Syria?" she asks me with attentive eyes.

I am momentarily speechless. The way she asks me… like she is genuinely curious. She doesn't ask with hesitance or thinly veiled judgment, or vengefulness. She asks because she wants to know. Her eyes shine with excitement. No one's looked at me like this since I got back. No one but her.

She stares at me with a waiting, impatient look. I stutter, but even my childish mortification cannot stop this burning warmth that fills me up. Some of the hate and distrust towards Dad and everyone else gets shoved out of me as my heart makes room for this woman's unfettered warmth.

"Well, I… I stopped in Istanbul on the way there. I actually spent most of my time there. And I met this kid, Ameer, on the streets. He is-was a Syrian refugee, but he was completely alone. I tried to help him but…" the sentence hangs in the air and pollutes it, until it is harder to breathe.

It hangs in the air, but it finishes in my head, unsaid. …I failed and a little boy died because of it. Because of me. Her head tilts to the side as her eyes zoom in on me. I feel like I'm back in Dr. Agatha's office, the shrink Dad forced me to see after Mom died. I hated that look. Gabriela examines me like bacteria in a petri dish, and I feel just as small. A shadow of partially veiled pity looms over in her stare.

"How was Syria?" she asks.

I know Gabriela's only purpose is to divert the discussion away from Istanbul, but the mention of Syria shatters my weak semblance of a happy facade. My smile breaks until I am frowning, until my eyes burn with unshed tears.

"I never should've gone." My voice breaks and the words spill out of me before I can halt them.

"What do you mean? Why not?"

I close my eyes briefly, but I don't see the millions in Syria. I see only the face of one. A little child, huddled against a street corner, alone. But he didn't have to be alone. I could've been his family, his friend.

There is nothing I can do to stop the wave of nausea that overcomes me, so I offer a hasty excuse to leave. I can't remember what I say, but none of this matters when I rush out of my boss's office to the bathroom. I throw myself against a stall door and my hands lock it. I hear my heavy, shallow breaths. The whooshing sound of an air conditioner. The faint trembling of the stall door that holds my weight. I see the bright lights of the nursing home bathroom under my closed eyelids. I feel my frantic heart racing, the churning of my empty stomach, burning with acid. I gasp for air, for an answer, for forgiveness, for the pain to go away. I'm feeling too much too soon and I just want it to go. I wish I'd never gone to Istanbul, never signed up for that relief trip. I wish I'd never met Ameer, because nothing is worth feeling like this.

I stay in the bathroom until my heartbeat slows and my hands stop shaking.

I ignore the tingling in my fingers as I wash my hands. The freezing water takes away some of the fatigue. I pat my hands dry on my scrubs and push open the bathroom door. And then I take a deep breath and do what I do best. Ignore what I feel to do what I must. My one talent.

Chapter Forty Five

I walk into Mary Parker's room with a tall glass of water and pills in hand. She's one of the newer patients that transferred while I was away. She's looking out the window when I walk in, and doesn't notice me until I speak.

"Ms. Parker?"

She turns to me, startled. Frail white hair frames a wrinkled, tired face. Her eyes are a muddy brown and chapped lips are spotted brown. She wears thick rimmed brown glasses that are unfit for her small, skinny face. Plain. Forgettable.

This is what I think of her as I smile plainly and set her meds on her nightstand and hand her the glass of water. But she doesn't notice my outstretched hands as her eyes light up and looks directly at me.

"Don't sneak up on me like that! I'm old, silly things like that can kill me, y'know?"

Stunned, I apologize to her by habit. She grabs the water from my hands and it sloshes from the cup. She mutters back at me, and her words remind me of a badmouthed teen, not a senior citizen at a nursing home. I can't decide if she's fire-spirited or just mean. I decide on the latter. As I leave her room, she calls me back and motions for me to come back with impolite, stiff hand gestures.

"Yes?" I ask, as politely as I can manage.

"Get me somethin' to eat. Haven't eaten since break-fast," she mutters.

I take a deep breath. "We'll be serving lunch at 11:30. That's... only two hours away. Would you like to wait for the meal?"

She stares at me like I'm stupid and offending. I hope I don't mirror it. "Yes, I mind. I'm hungry and expect to get food when I ask for it. God, this place costs my son an arm and a leg, and you people can't even get me a simple meal when I ask for it." Her monologue is followed by some foul language that makes me blush in both embarrassment and anger. What is this lady's problem?

"I didn't mean to offend you. Forgive me. Yes, I can get you something to eat. I'll bring a menu." I turn on my heels and rush for the door but she calls me back.

"Did I say I needed a menu? Just go and make me one of those turkey sandwiches. And put some hot sauce in it. And extra salt. Everything here tastes like cardboard."

I fist my hands and squeeze. I feel my patience teetering, and now, I'm not so sure I want to keep my temper in check. It would be so nice to just let it go for once. But the reasonable, innate part of my brain pulls me back.

"I'm afraid we don't offer that. How about I show you the menu and you can pick something from--"

"A turkey sandwich? You can't make me a turkey sandwich? Jeez. Forget it. I'll just starve till lunch. And what you gonna give me then? Huh?"

I turn around at turtle's pace now. I turn and stare her dead in the eye. I move closer until I hover over her.

"First of all, I'm a nurse with a college degree. Not some waiter or personal maid for you. Second, I'd appreciate if you didn't talk down to me like you've been doing ever since I walked in here. And finally, your son pays good money for this place because the nurses here are top notch and are part of the top ten nursing homes in America."

I feel a brief moment of dark satisfaction creep into every crevice and nook inside me. But it vanishes as fast as it came when I turn. And meet my boss's face.

Her eyes burn into me until my face feels hot, my shirt is sticky with sweat, and my heart pounds against my chest. The stare of death only lasts a moment, but my body doesn't calm until much after.

She walks close to me and rounds the bed. Then she smiles at Mary Parker with her placating, plastic smile. It fools everyone.

"Ms. Parker, hello. I'm not sure what got into Ms. Whitaker over here, but I sincerely apologize for her inappropriate behavior. "

Mary looks pleased with someone bowing at her feet, but she quickly replaces it with an unsatisfied snooty look.

"I want her gone."

"There will definitely be consequences for her. Again, I'm so sorry for her words. This place is not only a clinic, but I hope to make it feel like a home. We want everyone to feel welcome and have their needs met. Today, I broke my promise to you. For that, I am truly apologetic. Is there anything at all we can do for you to fix this?"

She looks nowhere at all for a moment in deep ponderment. And then she looks up with this almost innocent look.

"Well, you could get me a turkey sandwich?"

Chapter Forty Six

Property Brothers plays on the staticky small flatscreen. The curtains move in abrupt fluid movements. I lay down on my beige leather couch, legs across the armrest and eyes closed. I can smell the acidity of the air outside my apartment, where it always smells like gas is leaking. I hear the air conditioning creaking and whooshing. And underneath my closed lids, I see the flickering luminescent lights of my living room. And then I feel my white shirt still sticky from sweat. And finally, the tears, now cold, on my cheeks, feel icky. Some slide onto my lips and I taste metallic salt.

I don't know who I'm crying for, or even why. I still have my job, despite a furious boss, and I'm at home watching Property Brothers with a bowl of ranch seasoned popcorn and Cherry Coke. The closest a shy girl like me gets to heaven. Except it isn't. My life is in a whirlwind that only I can see, and therefore, I'm the only one who can catch it. But I can't do it. I'm so unsure. I don't know what to do. I don't know who to be. I don't know what to believe.

I think about Ameer, as I always do when these tears are prompted. But this time, I think about his past. What had that boy been through? What did he suffer? I think about what his parents looked like. Did he have siblings? Friends? What did he want to be? Did he like to read? Did he know how to read? Was his family rich? Poor? I know nothing about him, and yet I feel so much for him. I feel so much for what could've been. For what I could've become. I could've saved someone's world, and yet I left anyway. Myself, me. Me, me, me. Is that all I think about?

I scrub the tears off my face and sit up abruptly. For the first time I can remember, I am disgusted with myself. I feel repulsed for my self-centered thinking, my self-pity, and my selfishness. I'm so selfish.

And now, a little boy pays the price. A little boy lost the rest of his life, the rest of his possibilities. He could've had infinity and I cut it short. Because I took the easy way out.

Muffled shouting brings me back to the present. The neighbors are at it again, and the noise clouds my apartment. Slowly, my house feels smaller and smaller until I feel like I'm suffocating. The musky smell of gas burdens the densening air, and the flickering lights become constricting. The red fleece blanket feels too heavy, too hot.

I toss the blanket off me and replace it with my beige trench coat that is only a couple inches short of touching my ankles, so that only the tips of my plaid pajama pants show. And then those get covered too with knee length brown boots.

I take a peak in the mirror and see how ridiculous I look. The thick Nike hoodie makes me look fat and my hair is a brown bird's nest. I tie it into a low pony and grab my purse and keys. And then I lock my brown wooden door. The incessant fighting gets louder once I'm in the hall, but the promise of fresh midnight air makes it bearable. I hold my breath through the clogging cigarette smoke that seeps from an apartment room. And then I'm outside and all of that fades.

The sky is so blue it looks black, and I only notice the stars when I look for them. But once I do, they are bright. I get in my car, shivering. The air is still tainted by smoke and gas, and my hands are ice, but at least I can breathe. At least I'm here.

I shift gears and back out of the parking space. I drive out of the apartment complex and reach a green light. Then I'm out into the wide world, and I am alone, driving. I drive and drive and drive. I burn gas on the highway, and I consider stopping at one of the parks, but my better judgment decides against that and keeps me on the road. So I keep driving, until I am in the city and illuminating street lamps replace the stars. Until deserted roads are replaced by a million pedestrians, cars, and yellow cabs.

I find a bookstore coffeehouse that looks quaint and inviting. I park my car and climb out onto filthy, faded grey streets. The air is clouded here too, but it is warmer from crowded bodies. When I walk into the store, a warm gush of air greets me. The air smells like vanilla beans, used books, and coffee. String lights hang where the high ceiling and walls meet. The cream colored walls mostly hide behind framed whimsical pictures and vintage, pastel colored decorations. To my left, there is a black wooden coffee bar. A black chalkboard displays the menu, and I read fancy names of different teas and coffees I don't recognize. The lighting is dimmer there, with low hanging light bulbs. But everywhere else I look, I see books. Plain white bookshelves that barely miss the ceiling are stuffed with books, and the colored spines bring life to the bland colors of the store. My chest widens as my spine be-comes straight. Here, my worries disappear. Here, I feel potential. I feel free.

Gone are the burdening chains of guilt and worry. I feel light and I feel peace envelop me like a cozy bear hug. The only thing I am certain of is my uncertainty. Everything else hangs in the air, and that doesn't change, no matter how many Christmas lights and books and coffee I surround myself in. But for the first time, I'm okay with it. I have none of the answers, and I don't think I'll ever have all of them all at once. But what I have here, in the now, is enough. Because it has to be.

My chest rises and falls slowly now, and my strides are dragged out. I don't have all the time in the world, but tonight, I'll let myself be free.

I go to the coffee bar and the waitress greets me as soon as my hands settle on the black marble counter-top. She asks me what I want, and I tell her I have no idea. She laughs, and for a moment, I'm jealous of how certain she looks. Her hair is midnight blue and personally, I don't think she's the prettiest girl I've seen. Her nose is a little too wide, her lips too thin, her blue eyes too narrow. She's skinny like a twig, too skinny. I feel like if I touch her, she would snap.

Nothing about her is just right, and yet, she seems content with herself. Or maybe she's not, and she's just really great at what she does. Maybe she's just as screwed up and unsure and pained as the rest of us. As me. Or maybe she really is happy, and maybe her life is perfect, or it's completely screwed up, and she's still happy. Maybe, maybe, maybe. By the time she recommends one of the coffees after I tell her how I like my coffee (plain and strong), and I order what she recommends, I almost ask her. And then she's gone, and I'm left wondering. Maybe it's better this way. I'll never know her story, and she'll never know mine. Just two strangers in passing.

As I wait for my drink, I wonder why I keep wondering. I always have questions, which would be fine if I didn't always expect answers. Most of life's wonders and horrors are mysteries and maybe I should start being okay with that. Maybe I should stop trying to find all the answers. Maybe I should stop trying to fix everything, and just fix what problem comes to me.

Angie, the waitress, brings my coffee in a white porcelain mug. I thank her with half a smile and sit on one of the black cushion bar stools. As I finger the rim and stare at the white heart design on my coffee, I think about Ameer. I think about what I did, and I finally admit I was wrong. I should have stayed with Ameer. I should have saved him, and I know that now. I know I made a fatal mistake, but I also know that it's over, and no matters how many tears I cry, no matter how angry I get, no matter how much I wish he was coming back, he isn't, and he never will. My heart aches and I hunch over my mug. It hurts to know the truth, but as I close my eyes, I feel something lighten inside my chest, and I know once the pain finally fades from the forefront into background, I will get my peace. It will come in sporadic bursts and not all at once, but it will come. And as it does, I must do something worth doing. I may have failed Ameer, but there are more than seven billion people on the planet. I will figure out how to help at least one. And this time, I'll do it because I should. Not for me. For them. And for him.

Chapter Forty Seven

I tentatively sip my coffee. It burns my tongue, and it is also bitter and burnt and… fruity. Two packets of sugar later, and it still tastes strange to me. I don't like it, but I drink it anyway, in small regretful sips. After a few more minutes of this, I move to the sugar and cream counter, and transfer my drink into a to go cup. I snap on a lid, and then I go off to the bookshelves and wander.

The books are ghastly disorganized. I can just imagine the horror on Ms. Brenda's face, my elementary school librarian. I laugh to myself as I imagine the old woman's expression. Well, now that I think of it, Ms. Brenda wasn't actually old. She had jet black hair, paper white skin, and an average height and build. Late twenties, mid thirties- she was almost my age. I suppose to an eleven year old, thirty is old. I remember thinking when I was in second grade, I think, that when I would reach twenty, I would be wise and well-off. Then, I would be happy. And why not? No more spelling tests, or chores, or sharing a bunk bed with Abby. I remember thinking that happy would be definite if all I had was my own house, my own car, and me. Maybe a couple friends and a husband to have my happily ever after with. A few children running around. I almost snort. Fat chance of that happening.

All that was my equivalent of a white picket fence, house on the hill dream. And for the most part, I got it. I could've had the husband, but I was too scared to make anything sure. To put my heart into anything I couldn't control. Just so scared of ever feeling, of vulnerability. I'm still stupid and young and if I'm lucky, I'll learn much more. But I am wiser than I was when I was ten, wiser than I was even a few months ago. And I'm finally learning that all love and happiness comes with the price of uncertainty. Again, I think of my affection for Ameer. At times, it feels like jumping off a cliff into darkness, with no promise of a net, or anything else to catch me. And the sad thing is, sometimes we fall and there isn't a net. Sometimes we fall and smash into unforgiving concrete, and sometimes, it breaks us. I know this after losing my mother and then again losing someone dear to me, Ameer. And now, too, with my father. I feel like I'm losing him, with each meeting, each conversation. He slowly slips further from me and closer to something dark and unacceptable. He's called and texted, but I don't respond. And then I do and I feel guilty for not answering all those times and answering just that once. I hate talking to him now. But I can't give up on him. Maybe I'll fail, and maybe not. None of that matters. He's my father, and I love him. I won't quit on him, too. Not after Ameer. Not after Mom.

As I scan worn spines of books I'll never read, I realize something that makes me smile. I am uncertain of one less thing. And for now, that's enough.

Chapter Forty Eight

By the time I am in bed, it is well past midnight. I can still faintly taste toothpaste and that fruity coffee I couldn't finish. My hands grip the worn, dark blue covers printed with green and gold paisleys. I bury my face into my pillow and my long curls tickle my cheeks. And then I shift to my left and the sheets wrap around my body like a cocoon. I feel a little jittery from the too late caffeine. I close my eyes for two short seconds until they pop open again and I am wide awake. Twenty agonizing minutes later, I spring up from bed and quit on sleep. It's close to one now, but somehow, I don't feel worried. In fact, I feel like I'm floating on a cloud. I guess getting a revelation can do that to a person. That, or Angie's Americano had something a little stronger than caffeine in it.

I shiver in my oversized college t-shirt as I turn on the lights after walking into my closet door, and then I pull on my plaid pajama pants. They're cool from lying on the floor, and another shiver runs through me, so I wrap myself in my puffy turquoise robe. I'm still not sure if it's a house robe or a bathrobe, but it's warm and fleecy, and way too old to return.

My feet paddle loudly against creaking floorboards to the dark kitchen. I skim the wall for the light switch and flip it on, and the sudden light makes my eyes squint and burn. Peaking through my lashes at the floor, I go to the coffee maker and get a cup, coffee, and sugar. I start the coffee maker, and as it brews, I walk to the other side of the room and stare at the bookshelf. My hands reach for the prettiest spine, one with brown leather with gold trimming, and I look at the cover before settling the book on the top of the bookshelf to keep it to read once the coffee is finished. I'm not an avid reader by any means, but I used to be when I was in college and high school. But tonight, I have the burning urge to pick up a book and read. Maybe it's from entering a magical bookstore for the first time in a while. It felt like I entered Narnia tonight, and maybe this sudden need for a book of my own is my desperate attempt to recreate just a sliver of the magic in the shop. But, for a moment, I close my eyes and breathe.

I hear the coffee churning and groaning after years of use. A whispering breeze chills my skin and I shiver. But the wind doesn't seem like it is aimed for me. In fact, I feel like I am blocking the path of it, and segments of the wind rush into me by chance. This sudden possibility makes me feel small and finite in a never ending, ever encompassing universe. My body relaxes like melted butter and sways with the breeze, rather than against it.

The churning sound slows then stops, and the abruptness of the sudden lack of noise brings me out of my reverie. Breathing deeper now, with a slower stride, I walk to the coffee machine with slightly squinted eyes. Yawning, I fill my red and yellow striped mug. It's ugly and old, but somehow, coffee never tastes as magical as it does when I drink it from anywhere but here. I'm almost sure all of that is a load of crap, but it's nice to have something quirky to fall back on. Something solid, even if it's just a facade. Because really, there isn't anything anyone can rely on. No person, no money, no mug.

I add a spoonful of sugar, and then I put everything

away. As I reach for the bag of coffee, the mug tips and scalding drink spills all over me. In my rush to clean the mess and cool my burns, I push my mug off the counter. One second, it's rolling on the counter, and then it's on the floor in one thousand unsalvageable shards. My heart chips and my forged magic vanishes. I want to scream and cry and whine, but I just stand there with quickly cooling drink on my pajamas and robe, next to spilled coffee and broken glass. I stare at it, willing for the mess to disappear. When my impossible wish fails to come true, the whining voices in my head crank up their volume. And then all quiets except this one voice. One word. Quit.

And I almost do. I almost leave the kitchen with the lights on, the coffee pot on, the coffee dripping from the counter, the ugly mug in chunks and crumbs. I almost leave everything and go to bed and stay there whatever happens next. I wasn't thinking that far. Not that any of that matters, because I never go to bed that night. Instead, I find the dust pan under the sink and sweep up the mug. Then I wipe the counters and floor with a wet cloth, and then a dry one. I turn the coffee pot off and toss the rags onto the table and turn off the kitchen lights and find my way to the couch. I sit, back hunched, frowning. I think about calling it a night and going to sleep, but something tells me I won't be able to tonight. So out of habit, I turn on the TV. The harsh light illuminates the room in a depressing kind of way, or maybe everything looks gloomy right now. I flip through the channels aimlessly,and I reach a news channel and I'm about to move onto the next when I see the headline. Fire in Jordan Kills 12.

I am wide awake now, and lean forward with a frantic heart. My legs uncross and I sit at the edge of the couch, turning up the volume. The news anchor tells me a refugee camp was bombed. Seven of the victims were children.

Everything after that is just noise, from the lady's remorseful speech that seems less than sincere, to the vacuum commercial. I see images flit across the screen and a man's cheery voice. There's something about sale prices and free delivery. I hear tidbits without listening. My mind is somewhere else that is far, far away from here. Eventually, I fall back onto the couch and close my hurting eyes. My heart hurts and the next thing I do is imagine what that fire looked like. Flames, smoke, burnt buildings, dead people. Women and children. Screams of agony and cries of loss. The burning, painful smell of smoke. Of burning flesh. Of pain. Of hopelessness. Entire tents, unsafe havens gone. These people's little amount of food, clothes, pieces of their last home turned to ash. I imagine mothers clutching their children in their arms with splotchy tear stained faces that may never smile again.

The news comes back on and the bearer of bad news grins now with pearly whites, telling me about a victory for a college basketball team for one, a loss for another. And then underneath, a stream of less important news flows in small red print. I pay attention to one of them. Fire in Jordan kills 13 and 30 injured.

My heart throbs uncomfortably, but is familiar to me now, and I'm not sure how to feel about that. But this fleeting thought disappears in a haze of anxiety and pain and complete uncertainty. I turn my head and my eyes search for the coffee pot and I come up empty handed in the dark shadowed room. But this apartment is familiar, and I can picture where it sits on the counter, and my eyes stay fixated on a black blob where I know my coffee maker is. I think of the small loss of one mug that I was emotionally attached to. How would I feel if I lost this whole apartment? My home? I complain about the cramped space and bland walls and emptiness, but I know I would remember this place fondly if I ever lost it. And I know I'm lucky to have it right now. I know this, and yet, I rarely remember to feel grateful.

When I saw the refugee tents in Syria, my first thought was how sorry I felt for the inhabitants. My second thought was how thankful I was to not be among them. And here I sit, on my couch with a heated apartment and a stocked kitchen and a bed and job and a family, albeit not the best one, yet one nonetheless. I have all this that others would only dream of. I know that now. Or maybe I always knew, but I never cared until I saw it with my own eyes. At first, I am angered at all the ignorant people that surround me, and then I burn from shame, because until recently, I was one of them.

But I'm not so ignorant anymore. People say day-dreamers are in their own world, that they live in fantasies. Intangible and fake, as is mine. Until tonight, I thought living in my own world was something I was entitled to, but no one is. I can't stick myself in a bubble and live as if I am the only one who exists. My entire life, I've wondered how everything and everyone fits into my world, and I'm always bitterly disappointed. I kept thinking all else was a piece in my puzzle. I am a microscopic piece in a wide, wide world.

My life isn't just about me or my fulfillment. I am a lake that spills into the ocean. And so far, my current is low. But that's about to change.

Chapter Forty Nine

I wake with an aching back and a stiff knot in my neck. I feel I haven't slept at all, and yet, I precede my alarm by thirty minutes, and I spend it lying back on the couch and thinking about last night and the day ahead. I find myself doubting my promise to make my life about others, and think it might be a fluke. But fluke or not, it's the only thing that gets me off the couch and into the bathroom, ready to face the world through a different lens. I remember thinking last night, imagining how this morning would go. I saw myself getting up early and fresh, with plenty of time and motive to shower as I hum to crappy music, and then wear clean crisp shrubs with flawless makeup. Winged eyeliner, maroon lipstick, the works.

But my morning isn't nearly as picturesque. I waddle to the bathroom on knocking knees and tingling feet, and shower in lukewarm water because the tubes need fixing, and I develop a cold as I climb out, shivering. My clean scrubs are tumbled in a pile on my bedroom floor, and I have to get out my iron from the back of my closet to get out the wrinkles.

My hand slips as I put on eyeliner and I have to redo it twice, and my final attempt is thick and uneven. I hunt for my favorite ruby lipstick, and find it under my nightstand after a long search. My scalp stings and throbs from roughly brushing out the huge knots since I ran out of conditioner.

But when I leave the house, I look a little better than yesterday. I even manage a stop by Pete's to get my favorite chocolate chip muffin and espresso. I open my windows and turn up the nauseating country music from the radio to the chilly March air. At a red light, a middle aged scruffy looking man is holding up a cardboard sign asking for money. His tangled ginger hair reaches the middle of his back and his jeans and shirt are stained and torn. His shoes are worn and his teeth match the color of coal. I've ignored him for the past three days, imagining him using my money to get high, or for a smoke. As if I know a thing about this man's story, to justify my stinginess, but today, this ends. I give him ten dollars and a timid smile. Moments before, I had planned what I would say, but none of that matters because no words come out. Maybe that's for the best, because sometimes, silence outweighs words. The man doesn't smile back. He just nods and I see him swallow hard. And then the light turns green and I am off to work. And he is back to standing on a street intersection to beg for money. For what, I can never be sure of. But I don't think that matters. It's not about their intentions, it's that he asked for help and someone must give it. And now I'm deciding that person is me.

This feeling is new and a bout of warmth inflates my

lungs. I remember graduating and starting my career as a nurse, because more than anything, I wanted to have a positive impact. I remember being good. I get faded memories of the girl I was. Imperfect, struggling, but good. And then somewhere along the line, I got lost and when I found something to gravitate back to, I became the center of my universe. And the rest of the wide, wide world faded into background. But I think Ameer spun my world out of control, and I became disoriented again, and when I found my way again, I got back my strive for goodness.

I park five minutes earlier than my usual time. As I walk into the building, I know where my first stop will be: Mary Parker's room. I must apologize, even if it means swallowing my pride. Yes. Even then.

But when I walk, a miserably familiar sight greets me. A coroner, two crying women, and an awkward blonde haired boy who fidgets. My boss runs around and solemn nurses follow her barking orders. And finally, the white sheet that conceals the lady I yelled at like a lunatic only yesterday. I try halfheartedly not to hate myself as someone bumps into my shoulder and yells an apology. But I want to hate me, because don't I deserve every bit of guilt that swarms me and burdens my shoulders until they hunch over? I stare at the crying family and my heart chips.

The rest of the day is hazy and exhausting. I forget about my muffin and coffee, and then I don't take a lunch break because work is too hectic. By the time the clock hits four, my stomach is growling painfully and my eyes droop.

Chapter Fifty

A warm spring breeze greets me on an April morning. It is a peculiar surprise after an eternity of freezing days. Today is the first day of the month, and I decide to view it as a new beginning. A new month means a new opportunity. A short time ago, I hated to sound anything like those glass-half-full people. But as nauseating as it sometimes seems, it is also refreshing. Everything is so much better if seen in a forgiving light.

I wake up promptly at eight. My sweaty winter pajamas are the first to go and I dress in cool clothes and fresh springy colors. After, I make coffee and buttered toast, and watch the news while eating on the couch. Once I finish my toast, I mute the TV and get my laptop, and the metal cools my sweating hands. I turn on the fan and pull my hair up. The heavy material of the couch is too hot so I move to the kitchen counter and sit on a stool. I drink my warm coffee as I wait for the Syrian donations page to load, and when it finally does, I donate my usual amount, and some of my sharded bitterness evaporates. I heard once that giving away money is the only way money buys happiness. I never bothered listening until now. My phone rings from an unknown number, so I answer it tentatively.

"Hello?"

"Good morning, Ms. Whitaker! I'm Matt from the Trump campaign. How are you today?"

My knee burns and I see brown black liquid dripping

from my mug. "The… the Trump campaign? How did you get this number?"

"Oh… well, since you voted for Mitt Romney last-"
I am about to tell him that he got the number wrong. But then I remember my Dad. He used this phone for a while, and he must have put it down when he voted for the guy. Why am I surprised? I shouldn't be. Romney's not a bad guy, and he's a rich guy's hero. No, that's not the problem. It's why he didn't vote for the other guy.

I don't bother explaining all this to the phone man. Instead, I tell him to continue while simultaneously imagining a thousand things to yell at my father. He might as well get an orange tan and start saying "bigly" as if the words exists.

"-Wondering if you wanted to volunteer for the Trump campaign to show your support. We are located at-"
I cut him off again, as it seems I'm on a roll today. "Do you hear my voice? You can tell I'm a woman, can't you?"

"Ma'am-"

"I also have this little thing called self-respect. So why the hell would I vote for that racist, sexist, arrogant pig?"

"Ma'am, I understand we all have our differences in opinion. But this is the future president of your country-"

I hang up.

Chapter Fifty One

I stand at the footsteps of Dad's house. I feel cold but there are no shivers, only goosebumps that harden my numb skin. I blow in shallow puffs and my rosy cheeks are warm. Unfiltered sunlight tingles my back and I feel shards of heat on my arms. When I left the house, I paid no mind to my sweat-pants and snug hoodie, because I was too busy being boiling mad. But now, some of my anger slips and uncertainty suffocates me.

I ring the doorbell and wait. What else can I do? People say there is always a third option, but this time, there is only option A or option B. A means running away and ignoring a problem that I have the potential to affect and a person to educate. B means ringing the doorbell and standing in skin I'm totally uncomfortable in, just so that I can touch at least one person's heart. My father's.

But then the maid opens the door and my courageousness flees. Then I'm standing in the over embellished fancy living room, feeling like a little girl again. Dad's unique thumping footsteps become louder until I turn around and face him. His greying cropped hair is wet, and his face is the color of paper, with the exception of tinged cheeks. He wears faded designer jeans and a plaid yellow and green shirt.

"Hey! Wasn't expecting to see this daughter anytime soon. How are you, kiddo?"

I smile awkwardly and return his hug. He smells like that blue cologne I always loved, and I feel a wave of calm wash over me. The smell is so achingly familiar that I feel a pain in my chest at old lies I miss believing in. I feel a strange nostalgia over what my world used to be and what it could never be again.

"Well... how are you?" I ask. We sit on the same cream colored leather sofa. The leather is cold against my skin, and I shiver.

"I'm good! My contract with the Bernstein couple just ended. I enjoyed that project, but glad to be done with it. Those people are a couple of rich, spoiled snobs. I hated them."

"Oh. Well... at least you're done with it."

"Yup. So, you want some coffee? I can start a pot."

"I never say no to coffee," I say as we walk to the kitchen. The thumping of our footsteps seems to echo in the big empty house. It feels lonely. Dad is rambling about a new project he's working on- there are cartoon vegetables involved- and he waves his arms and laughs in this animated, ridiculously childish way. And I feel my heart sink at how lonely he looks. I'm not the smartest, but I do know my family.

"Sugar?"

"One, please."

"Cream?"

"No thanks."

He hands me a cartoon illustrated mug, one that he designed. I sit on a bar stool and watch him pour a second cup. He adds two spoonfuls of sugar and a big splash of cream. He notices me cringing and laughs. It sounds sad, though. Forced.

"So, how are you?" I ask.

"You already asked me that."

"No. I mean how are you?"

He stares at me and laughs again. But his eyes look alert and defensive. Shoulders hunched.

"I feel like I'm in a shrink's office, again."

"I worry about you. That's all."

He rolls his eyes. "You freak out over roadkill."

"Yes, and that's your fault too. Ever since that drive to Florida. That poor squirrel…"

"Nell, you were twelve! How do you even remember that? But, whatever. That's my point. You are a worry wart. The very definition. In fact, I bet if you looked up worry wart, there'd be a big fat picture of you right under it."

"Worry wart is two words. It's not in the dictionary. Actually, is it? Do you have a dictionary here? I could look it up."

He rolls his eyes again. I roll mine back.

He leans closer and smiles softly. "I'm a big boy, kid. I can take care of myself, okay? Don't worry so much."

With his words come that signature stubborn look. He's not going to budge. I'm well acquainted with that look. In fact, I've worn it numerous times myself, so I don't bother arguing.

"Okay."

He grins. "Good. So, what did you wanna talk about?" I sip my coffee in slow intervals. "Well, I wanted to apologize about how I acted the other day."

My words surprise both of us. I can count on one hand the number of times I've apologized, and it's not what

I planned to do. Before I came here, I didn't think there was anything to be sorry to him for. But I think I was wrong. My father may support a despicable man, but he is still my father.

And he deserves to be treated as so.

"You're... apologizing. Well, I'll be damned."

"Dad..."

"You didn't even apologize after you crashed my boat. In fact, when I grounded you, you got mad at me," he says incredulously. My face heats up in sheer mortification after being reminded of who I was. And who I desperately try not to be.

"Yeah, well. I'm trying to change that. So... sorry."

He stares at me with this look I don't understand. Maybe it's incredulity, disbelief, and knowing. Like he has my biggest secret that even I am unaware of. I don't like it.

"Okay."

I feel my eyebrows rise to my receding hairline. "Okay? That's it?"

"I mean, okay. You're forgiven. It's done. Over. Terminado. Moving on."

"Actually, there was something else I wanted to say."

"Sounds ominous."

It was, but I couldn't tell him that. So I say he's being ridiculous, and then I take a deep breath and start.

"I love you, Dad. Really. I know we don't always see eye to eye, but I always love you. It's just, that Donald Trump sign? Why?"

"Oh, not this again."

I sense a whiny rant coming, so I quickly interrupt.

"Please, Dad. It's important to me."

He sighs this very long, very heavy sigh and then nods. "So, why?"

"I like the guy. What's the big deal?"

"But why do you like him? He's arrogant and smug, and his smile is just plain creepy."

"I don't wanna marry him, Nell. And since when do you judge people based on how they look, anyway?"

It's my turn to sigh. "The orange thing was a joke. But the rest of it isn't. I wouldn't care if he was broccoli green with one eye, Dad."

"Really? Because I would. I like my presidents to have all their body parts. And maybe green is a bit of a stretch."

I roll my eyes again. Maybe Dad's rubbing off on me. That thought freaks me out more than graveyards on Halloween, so I push it away and decide to handle reality for now. "Seriously. Why do you like him?"

"Why don't you?"

"Dad."

"Fine, fine. You're stubborn as hell. Got that from your mother. Anyway. Um. I dunno. He's straightforward. He's honest. I like how he wants to go hard on fence jumpers. And I bet he'll lower taxes for us. That'll be awesome."

"But... but he's awful! The way he treats women, and how he's the biggest xenophobic I know. Oh, and don't even get me started on the wall.

"Okay, Nell. Just calm down. Stop yelling."

"I'm not yelling!"

Dad stares at me like I belong with Zelda Fitzgerald. I don't blame him. He tries to get another word in but I don't let him. I guess he's right about one thing. I am stubborn.

"You know, I don't even know why I bothered coming here. You're my dad and I wanted to believe I could understand where you could possibly be coming from. Because this isn't just about who you vote for this year. It's about what that implies. And... and I don't know how to accept it."

I look down and I see my green jacket is already on and I have my phone and wallet in hand. "I... I'm sorry. I have to go," I apologize out of habit. And then I leave.

Chapter Fifty Two

I don't feel like returning to an empty apartment, so I drive downtown instead. There is an abundance of quaint coffee shops there, and at the very least, there will be coffee and white noise to keep my head relatively empty.

It is only when I finally end the struggle of parallel parking that I realize I look like crap. I hunt for something to help make me look presentable. I come up with sparkly purple lip gloss and lemony lotion that makes my nose burn. I squirt some onto my hands anyway, and the lip gloss is not as girly as I expected, not that it puts a dent in my appearance. I laugh humorlessly at how ridiculous it is that I still care. Minutes ago, I was devastated about potentially destroying my relationship with my father, and yet, I worry about what people will think of my ragged appearance. I think I'll always care, and I'll always be disappointed because, undoubtedly, I will always fall short of what I expect to be.

I ignore the spiral of thoughts because I know I'm losing perspective. Dr. Barnes, my psychiatrist in high school, would tell me not to contemplate big life choices when I'm this upset. I ignore this rule too often. I get out of the car and double check to see if it's locked. I guess worry makes for good distraction.

No matter how many times I come here, I am always surprised by the beauty of the city. The shops are works of art composed of luminescent lights, cream colored walls, and black outlines. The air smells different too, like revitalization and pollution at once. Everything is always smaller than I expect, and there are so many people, all vastly different and yet so similar. I usually don't like big crowds but this doesn't feel like a crowd. Instead, it feels like a puzzle. Every piece contributes, and it fits together perfectly, and I am one small piece of the puzzle.

I don't have to walk far until I spot a coffee shop. The name, Ana's Brewery, sits atop the door in pretty black calligraphy blocks. The shop is well lit, and the windows take over almost the entire wall. There are bursts of forest green plants, and there is a fair number of people inside, but it doesn't look overwhelming, and there are no barking dogs, which I'm relieved by. The thought of dogs reminds me of the ones in Istanbul. They were huge, almost the size of wolves, but they were so calm and still. They walked leisurely, and once they sat, they seldom moved. They seemed almost mature, like many years of living had given them wisdom.

I pull open the glass door and only the delicate whoosh of air is heard. No creaking or thumping, but maybe the chatter drowns out the noise. I'm worried people will stare because of my sloppy appearance, but no one notices me. If they do, then they smile or nod. I feel relief, and then I am embarrassed. I think so little of these people, and I am so insecure.

I order a small lemon honey ginger ale and a blueberry scone despite my nausea. As I wait for my order, I look around. The store is rather spacious, despite the cramped tables and many people. I choose a booth in the far corner inside once I pick up my order. The brown leather is cold but soft. The table is the color of sand and feels like cold wood. A college girl a few tables left from me yells into a phone while her hands flail everywhere. A middle aged couple sits a few tables from her, and it looks like an awkward conversation. There are a few other people on laptops, buried in stacks of paper around me. Watching the world around me gives me a certain calm. The world seems bigger and my perspective widens. It distracts me from my own problems and I get to forget myself in everyone else's world. It's like reading an adventure or watching a movie. Maybe that's why I like TV shows so much; I get to focus on someone else's story so it distracts me from my own problems. And wherever Derek Shepherd is involved, I must be too.

As it often does, my mind shifts to Ameer. I miss him

more than I expect myself to, but maybe it's not only him I miss. I miss the prospect of a life with him, and the chance to change someone else's life as drastically as Ameer changed mine. Whenever I gave him food or clothes or that kite, I thought it was him who was lucky to have me, but I was gravely wrong. I was the one who gained the most from giving to Ameer, because he gave me much more. He made me thankful and humble and decent. I just wish I realized that sooner so that I would've had the sense to save him. Dr. Barnes would tell me not to dwell on the 'what ifs', but I ignored that advice because I thought I deserved the pain. Maybe I do, but that's no way to live and I'll never be able to make my life worth anything if I don't get past it. In think a part of me will always regret leaving Ameer, but I can't spend any more nights on it. I can't.

I think about my wish to help. I feel a certain obligation to the children of Syria. I feel there is an unwritten part to my story that I must write. And this chapter will be how I help the children of Syria. However, I have no money of mine to spare for funds or another trip to Syria. And even if I could, I don't think I could handle it. I came back early last time for a reason, and I'm not keen on revisiting. But there must be something else I could do. Even if I don't have the money, I could raise funds. And maybe more than anything, I could make people aware. Certainly I'm not the only one who could be awakened. If we could only feel the suffering and loss of Syria, maybe then we would find our own way to help. It's a rather optimistic ideology, but I'm going to stick with it. I used to think optimism was idealistic, and therefore unrealistic. But miracles are just as real as devastations. Optimism is real, because good things happen. I need to find it in me to believe in that again. This is my first step.

Chapter Fifty Three

I stay at the shop only to finish my coffee. And then I leave and drive home. When I enter my apartment, the quiet feels peaceful, but it is still lonely, no matter how much I deny it. My thoughts drift to Dad and I expect anger. But there is only remorse, and maybe guilt. I tell myself to believe in people, and yet I can't even give my father the chance to surprise me. But I'm learning.

I'm still reeling from the events with my father, and I decide to avoid action or talking until I feel more put together. Whatever that means. Until then, I will plan this… well, whatever this is. I can pull together a birthday party, but a fundraiser is a different story. I do know someone who specializes in this very thing: Abby. I almost dismiss the thought because of all the horrific scenarios I conjure up, but I remind myself not to be harsh on the prospect of possibility. And maybe this will be an opportunity to reconcile with my sister. She's not perfect, but no one is. It's why I could never get close to anyone. Under a magnifying glass, everyone has a few repulsive traits and thoughts and secrets. Everyone does, including me. I must not be so harsh on anyone, or I'll remain alone and hateful forever.

I've never tried reaching out to her in such a direct and huge way before, but I decide it's what I'll do. And however it turns out, something good must come of it. But I'll know I'll find a million reasons not to do this if I wait even before tomorrow morning's coffee finishes brewing, so I send a short text asking her to meet me tomorrow. I draft it about a hundred times, though. The first few have a date and time included, but I force to take them out. I leave it open ended so it'll be on her terms. It's a struggle to let go like this, even for something as small as lunch plans, but I manage. And then I work another few million drafts until I get it just casual enough where it sounds relaxed and friendly, but not so much I sound aloof and uncaring. It all feels awkward and unnatural, but I force my way through it and send the message.

By the time I'm ready for bed, I see a reply. She agrees to meet me with an abundance of emojis, a bunch of exclamation points, and a suggested time and place. It's this strange breakfast diner I've never heard of before, but I can just imagine it'll be the kind of place that doesn't have prices on the menus, with about a dozen forks for each person. I just know it. And goodness, seven thirty in the morning? Does she not know me at all?

My thoughts only spiral downhill from there, so I force myself to focus on the one positive note. At least she agreed. Which isn't really positive, since I kind of knew she'd say yes. She's pretty eager to reconnect and all, or at least she acts so. I can never tell the difference with her.

But I send an affirmative response, with an added exclamation point and grinning emoji that makes me vomit. And once I hit send, I set an alarm for six, put my phone on the nightstand, and sleep.

Chapter Fifty Four

I snooze my alarm twice, and I almost call to reschedule. I groan dramatically as I tumble out of bed with a heavy head and sore back. I've never been drunk before, but I imagine this is what a hangover feels like.

Once I've showered and brushed, I stare at my open wooden closet, clueless. There is a heap of clothes on my bed that I continually toss in a slew of uncertainty. What does one wear for a breakfast with my sister? The restaurant is most definitely not a jeans-type place, so I mentally discard my many pairs. I think about my black slacks and a blouse, but I feel like I should wear something more feminine, with frills and hemmed flowers. But since my closet is frills-free, I decide on a lavender blouse and a black skirt that reached mid thigh. I begin to wonder if I have any jewelry, but then I realize how ridiculous I'm being. I settle with my royal blue bracelet from Istanbul. It has this infinity sign that sparkles like gems the color of diamonds. It is the perfect irony too, since nothing ever lasts, and the diamonds are fake. Just like infinity. Then I slip on the black sun necklace from Dad. I don't know if it makes me feel better or worse, but I leave it on.

I hunt down my makeup and put on this sparkly eyeshadow, but I end up getting it on my black skirt because I wipe my fingers on them. I look in the mirror, and I know I look pretty. Feminine. Sweet. I have glitter on my face and my lashes are thicker and exaggerated. My lips are coated in a soft pink that is a subtle shade from my natural tone. It suits me, but it's just short of bubblegum pink and I hate it. I may look pretty, but I don't look like me. I wipe off the lip gloss and replace it with a tan colored lipstick. I still look stiff, but it's less so. And I'm running late, which I hate since being punctual is one thing I can usually manage, so I leave as I am, in black flats. I've tiptoed my natural comfort line, but heels would be Usain bolting past that line.

I follow my GPS nervously, and I miss a turn because of it. I get to the restaurant ten minutes late, and I hope that she'll be late too, because punctuality is one place she falls short in. But I see her silver Acura parked. It seems like a weird choice of a car for someone as bubbly and perky as her, like I expect a yellow buggy from my baby sister.

The restaurant looks quaint and cute. It's right on the edge of the city, not too far from Abby's house. The windows are huge, but in the sunlight, I can only make blurry outlines of tables and people. I take a deep breath and walk in. And then I almost tip over.

The tables are worn wood with matching chairs. The place is crammed with furniture, and there are cream colored leather booths near the windows. No line of forks for each person. In fact, there are smeared laminated menus and those trays with salt, pepper, ketchup, and mustard. I like it. And I'm not sure how I feel about that.

I look for Abby at the tables because she's always loved sitting right in the middle of the action, but when I don't see her, I move on to the booths and spot her in the farthest corner. I walk over and she spots me. She stands up with this dopey grin and glowing eyes.

"Nellie! It's good to see you."

I smile. "Same here." I'm not sure how much I mean that, and by the looks of it, neither does she. We sit down and I reach for a menu to keep my fidgeting hands busy.

"You sure look fancy. Cute though," Abby teases and my cheeks burn as I feel myself growing hot. She wears black jeans and a cotton white shirt, with brown sandals and minimal makeup. I look like I'm going to a business meeting next to her.

I was expecting place settings and a blazer suit. Not... this. How do I keep getting it wrong with family?

"Yeah... well. Thanks," I clear my throat after my voice squeaks.

She laughs, then an awkward silence follows. I speak the first thing that comes to mind. "So, I thought you preferred the tables."

"Yeah, but you prefer booths."

"Oh."

"Was I wrong?"

"Huh? Oh, no. I... I do prefer the booths. Thanks."

"Yup. So do you know what you want?"

"Hmm, not really."

"Well, I recommend the double chocolate chip pancakes and hot chocolate. They use real cocoa instead of that packaged stuff."

I stare at her, jaw dropped open. "You've eaten here before?"

"Oh, yeah! I eat her practically every weekend. I love this place, but it's pretty packed after tenish, so I always come around this time."

"Huh."

We don't talk much until after we order. I get buttermilk pancakes and black coffee while she gets double chocolate chip pancakes and hot chocolate. We share a side of bacon and hash browns. After the waiter takes our menus, I delve into business.

"So, I have a proposition for you."

Her eyebrows reach her hairline. "So, that's why you called." She sounds angry.

"I'm trying to reach out to you here. Yeah, there was a reason why I texted you, but I did text you, didn't I?"

"Only 'cause you were desperate," she mumbles, pouting.

I roll my eyes. "You're being childish."

"Whatever." She rolls her eyes back at me.

"I rest my case."

At this, I catch a glimpse of her dimples that only show when she smiles.

"Okay, fine. What's this proposition?" She says with a very dramatic sigh.

I'm fighting a smile myself. I missed this... bickering. My sister has her fair share of problems, and I have mine, but I missed this. I missed my sister, even if it might be temporary.

"Well... you're an event planner."

She gasps. "Really? I had no idea."

"Okay, smart-alec. Can I finish without you interrupting?"

"You may," she says in a mock solemn tone.

A laugh escapes me. "Okay. Well... you know how I went to Syria a couple weeks ago?"

She gives me a pointed look. "Right, you do. I was just... okay. Well, I wanted to start a fundraiser for Syria. For the children in specific. I haven't really figured out the minor details, or even the major ones. At all. But I guess I was hoping you'd help me figure it out."

She just stares. No words, no smile. Nothing. Just a long unblinking stare that begins to remind me of the doll in Chucke.

"Are... are you sure that's a good idea?"

I glare at her. The magic disappears, and I feel a sense of foreboding and heaviness upon us. I hear distant laughter and I hate it. What is there to possibly be happy about?

"I- I'm sure you have good intentions, but are you sure it's such a good idea to run an event like that here. In a place filled with racist white people?"

"People like you?"

I see her uncertainty flee from her face and burning anger and loosely concealed hurt replace it.

"No. Not like me. God, you're such a judgmental prick. And… and what do you mean like me? If I recall correctly, you were never bothered by the crap Dad spewed before your Syria trip. I never liked it, even though I had never seen those people with my own eyes, but you didn't seem to have a problem with it. So why don't you get off your pedestal because you are no better!"

"Well, if you never felt that way, how come you never said anything to Dad? Or to me? You could have."

"And I did. Not when you two were in the same room together, because I didn't feel like wedging our family apart, especially after Mom died. But I did talk to Dad. And I tried to talk to you, but God, if the almighty Penelope Whitaker doesn't want to listen, nothing can make her."

I gape like a fish, mouth opening to defend myself and closing because there is nothing to defend myself. Abby's right.

So I remain silent. We both do.

The food arrives, but I just pick at it with my fork. Abby attacks it, though. She's a nervous eater. I just sip my coffee in small regretful sips. It's too weak for me, like flavored water. I wish I'd made my own at home.

"I'm sorry."

I'm the one to apologize, and we both stare at each other in shock, equally surprised.

The hardness in her face falls and she sends me a small,

kind smile that warms me and my shoulders relax in relief, without my knowledge they were tense to begin with.

"I'm sorry too. I guess we both went too far."

I nod and smile, and then I pick up my fork and take a bite of my pancakes after drizzling blueberry syrup over it. I moan. "These are amazing!"

She laughs. "I told you, didn't I? Although I still don't understand the point of getting pancakes without chocolate. If there's an option that includes chocolate, why would you choose anything else? And blueberry syrup? That stuff tastes like those blueberries that come in a can for blueberry muffins."

"Oh, I love those. I always eat a few before putting them into the batter."

Abby scrunches up her face and I laugh. I like the sound of it.

We eat and bicker and eat some more. Once we're done with our pancakes, we push aside the plate and I cup my coffee mug around my hands, absorbing it's weakened warmth and wetting my hands from the condensation.

"If you don't want to, you don't have to. But I… I would really like it if you'd help me with this event. Not just because I know you're good at what you do, but because this really is something important to me. I'm trying to change. And I did reach out to you because I want to get you back in my life. I want to fix this."

My sister is predictable like a clock, but this time, I don't know what she's going to say, and I feel vulnerable. I don't like it.

She smiles at me and her eyes are a swarm of emotions. "That means a lot to me."

Her voice is lower than a whisper.

I clear my throat. "So, you'll help me?"

She laughs in this choked up sort of way. "Yes. Yes, I'll help you if that's what you want."

I grin.

"I can't wait."

Chapter Fifty Five

The week passes, and by the time Friday night rolls around, I am exhausted in every sense of the word. It's 6:30 PM and I'm slumped on my couch with a frozen pizza dinner on the coffee table, soda cans, and my warmest green blanket. I'm exhausted, but I'm happy. I feel something greater is coming. I know it is.

I told Abby I'd get back with her this weekend, the one after our breakfast last Saturday. I pick up my phone and contemplate calling her because I hate texting, when my phone buzzes.

Abby: Hey! How are you? Was wondering if you wanted to meet up this weekend so we can start planning your event.

I smile and text her back before I can talk myself out of it.

Penelope: Hi. I'm good. Do you want to just come over to my house right now? There's pizza.

She texts me back immediately with a few typos and emojis. I smile, but I'm frowning when she asks me to send her my address. Has it been so long? I text it to her, and try not to dwell. What matters is we're trying now, and it's working out.

I change into jeans and a sweatshirt, and I brush my hair and put on a headband. Then I get a can of Cherry Coke from an assorted soda cans box and stick it in the freezer. The chalky flavor makes me puke, but Abby's in love with it. I stick to the boring classic stuff like Coke and Ginger Ale. Even her soda preferences are cooler than mine, but I'm used to it. We've always been polar opposites, and she's always the fun end of the pole. I have frizzy chestnut curls, a few too many pounds on my stomach and thighs, and a plain Jane face. She's got natural red hair, gorgeous green eyes, and cute petite features. Where I'm just fat, she's curvy. While I'm awkwardly tall, she's elegant in her extra long legs and elongated neck. The only thing we can both agree on is shoes. Neither of us can handle heels on a daily basis. Heels are kind of like birthdays. Once a year, and there's always a disaster the morning after.

The doorbell rings and I pause whatever random reality TV show plays. I open the door and smile when Abby barges in.

"Nice place."

"What? You've seen it before."

"Well, yes. But the only thing I recognize is the couch, and that's only because it was like, the first piece of furniture here."

"Oh."

We look at each other and agree wordlessly not to bother dredging up the past. We go to the couch, and she grins when she sees pizza. I get the soda from the freezer and give it to her.

"You finally caved and agree this is the best thing ever?"

"No. I still think it tastes like cough syrup. I bought this pack of assorted soda cans."

"Oh. Wait, the cough medicine you always used to spit into the sink when you thought Mom wasn't looking?

I laugh. "Yeah. Except, I only got away with it once. You always used to tell on me and yell to Mom."

"It was from a place of love and care. I was worried about you."

"And because you could bribe our mother into letting you eat a Twinkie after you played goodie two shoes."

"You're right. It was mostly for the Twinkies."

We laugh and joke and eat for an hour. By 8:00, we're laying on the floor with pillows and an empty pizza box and more soda cans. Once we're done laughing and imitating Tom Cruise's awful acting, we think about Mom together. There are no pictures of her here, and few pictures at all to begin with. I don't like being reminded of change. I don't like feeling vulnerable and sad, but Mom deserves to be remembered. Abby softly offers to give me a few of the pictures of Mom and me she still has hanging around. Abby's also my opposite when it comes to photographs, and her walls are covered with them. At least from what I remember about her home,.

I accept her offer and after a few moments of silence, I clear my throat with a hard swallow and divert our attention to the reason Abby came. The reason we're laughing with each other instead of screaming and yanking hair. We owe quite a lot to this new cause. The fundraiser, which I still have very limited knowledge of what it will be and what it can be. I hope the two ideas can become one, instead of expectations separate from reality. For once, I want them to intersect. For once.

Abby turns to me and gives me this very business professional look. "Okay. So, the first thing I'll tell you is that whatever you expect this event to be, banish the thought. It's your first big scale event, and chances are, it'll evolve with time. Allow it to be fluid. Don't be rigid, or you'll never be satisfied. I'm not saying it'll fall short from expectations, because I usually far exceed it. But it will be different."

I just stare at my half empty mug and finger the lip gloss stained rim. And then I laugh. Laughter comes out in squeaky, sometimes silent, pieces. I feel Abby staring at me confused. She's right, I think. I am crazy. How couldn't I be? I laugh because I'm still learning through utter failures of expectations. And I laugh because Abby's little monologue applies to more than just this event. I just never noticed as so before. I always assume life falls short of expectations when it actually exceeds them, just in different capacities.

I'm still learning. And I think, the longer I search for

answers, the more questions I'll find. That would've driven me mad before, but now it seems beautiful. Unanswered questions are what make people think. Searching for truth is the most thought invoking process I've found. I get a thousand answered and a million more to find.

Chapter Fifty Six

Abby pulls out a stack of manila folders and we discuss advertisements, avenues, and color themes. I answer varying versions of "You decide" and "I don't know" for most of the questions. The only definite answer I provide is for color themes. I want orange and yellow, and Abby scrunches up her face in this very judgmental, snobby way. She shows me my the color choice on her laptop for a flyer, and I ask her what's wrong with it. She gives me another one of her looks and then messes with my colors and fonts. She makes me turn around until I'm done, to get the full effect, she says. I think she doesn't want my commentary. She gets it anyway, even with my back turned. After a few minutes of my attention only partially diverted by Property Brothers, and then a medicine ad that spends most of its time on its dangerous side effects she summons me back.

"What about this instead?" she asks in this very polite very patronizing tone. I roll my eyes and look at the screen. And then I'm silent because I hate admitting defeat. Her style is way cooler. The fonts are more fitting and don't look so abrupt, and the yellow and white theme is much more appealing. It's perfect, save for a few margin and border issues that I settled on. I point to them and she messes with the keys and none of it makes sense to me. All I know is that it's good I never bothered pursuing my computer designs class freshman year of high school. And it's perfect that Abby did.

"It's… good," I grudgingly admit.

She stares at me with wide, brighter green eyes. "Good? Please, this is freaking awesome. You're so lucky you have me." I roll my eyes and smile. We both know she's right.

"So, about payments. How does that work?"

"You mean costs for the event?"

"You know it isn't."

She turns to me and sighs. "You're not paying me. At least not in money. But in pizza and Cherry Coke… bring it," she grins goofily. But I know she's not joking.

"No. I'm not going to let you-"

"You're not letting me do anything. I won't accept your money. Now drop it, okay?"

"But-"

"Stop. I took this gig for two reasons. One, you're my sister and I'd do anything for you. Two, I care about this too. I don't want to get paid for doing this. Please, Nell."

We're silent and the sound of breaking walls from the TV fills the room and is just short of echoing.

"Okay. Okay, I won't pay you." My voice is hoarse and quiet, but Abby smiles and I know she heard me.

And then we're both silent until one of us makes

mention of how a twin's hair dye job is quite hideous. I don't remember the rest of that conversation. At least I wish I didn't. She leaves when the clock strikes midnight, and oddly, I'm sad to see her go. But I toss the pizza box and cans, shut off the TV, and go to bed. Tomorrow is going to be a long day. Or at least I hope it will be.

Chapter Fifty Seven

We meet at Alta Plaza Park a week later, at the top of the hill. The view is beautiful, but I can't seem to comprehend it at 7:00 in the morning. I didn't have time to get coffee because I snoozed my alarm much more than once. I wear jeans, an orange shirt, a baseball cap, and my favorite green jacket. I'm still shivering, but I don't notice the chills because I'm too busy regretting not stopping for coffee. And now Abby's late, as she always is, and I'm tired and crabby. I see her speed walking up the hill a few minutes later. She's ten minutes late, and I tell her this.

"Sorry. I stopped to pick up some breakfast."

"Oh. Well… thanks. How did you know I hadn't eaten?"

"Because you hate early mornings, but not as much as you love punctuality."

I don't bother with a response as I sip my drink and eat my blueberry bagel with plain cream cheese, warm but not toasted.

"One sugar, no cream. You remembered."

"Unfortunately, yes. You're coffee's disgusting by the way. I bet you didn't even like it like that in the beginning. I bet you were just too lazy to go the fridge just for creamer, so you stopped and drank without." I laugh and she takes it as an affirmative.

"Laziness at its finest."

"At least I know that 7:30 means 7:30."

"Sorry, sorry! I'm working on the whole punctuality thing."

We sit on the edge of the hill that overlooks the city. We eat in silence and look around us. A flock of pigeons scatter around us. Worn cement stairs are above and below us. I look at the mass of buildings. There are too many to count, and yet, each structure has it's unique style. There is a wide range of color, from typical beiges and greys, to orange and green and blue and yellow and red. And despite the difference in styles, all come together to create this beautiful city. The clouded purple and pink sky is the prettiest skyline and a perfect fit.

I see cars crowd the streets and the bridges. I see the Golden Gate Bridge that is the color of bricks. I see lights from houses and streets, mostly. And then there is that awakening scent of coffee and food carts. Salted pretzels and sweet toasted bagels. There is also the unmissable stench of smoke and dirt. The trees and plants freshen the air, but the smell lies underneath, faded. I hear the footsteps of pedestrians, barking dogs, creaky and slamming doors, and chatter. I hear the screeching of tires and the whooshing sound of wind and doors opening and closing. I hear the pigeons too, as they squawk and flutter their wings and hit the cement and grassy plains that converge with the sidewalk. There is an empty tennis court behind us, and pigeons rest on the metal fences of the structure.

I breathe in the beautiful air as I admire the city as a massive puzzle made of pieces like buildings and streets and lights and green and people. Oh, the people.

I turn around to see the stream of people. I find a new meaning to the word "stranger". I see each individual as potential. Each with their own story and advantages and tragedies. We share the same stories in different shades and wrappings. Yet, we all have our own stories to tell because we really are unique. I see a street of people and I see a forest of trees. All made of similar roots, branches, leaves, and trunks. And yet, each tree has its own arrangement of branches and leaves. Their own variation of browns and greens. Their own number of leaves. Their own kind of trunk and number of rings. Their own roots, in size and color and placement and arrangement. I see a street of people and I see a limitless reservoir of potential and beauty and horrors.

I don't realize Abby's staring at me until I turn to stare at her. She's smiling but I don't think she knows it. It's this crooked, sweet smile. The kind that tells a story. I think I know what it means, but I don't ask. I smile back, and then we return to our breakfast. Once we have empty brown paper bags and cups, we toss them and dust off the back of our pants. She pulls out a stack of flyers from a Ziploc bag. I smile and glare at them simultaneously. After a hair-pulling week of finalizing dates and places and times, after a week of fighting with the printer guy and having an embarrassing meltdown in front of my sister… After a week, we're finally here. My morning crankiness is a distant memory and I'm grinning now, although that might be the afterglow of coffee.

I take a stack of flyers and she offers me a tape dispenser. Then we talk about strategy and I decide to store my bossiness in the corner of my mind, and let my little sister tell me what to do. She's the event planner anyway. We start with the intersections and tape the biggest posters there. Then we split up and walk into dozens of cafes and bookstores and clothing shops, asking to put up signs in their stores. Many say yes, and many say no. I try not to take it personally, and only partially succeed. Or partially fail, as Abby tells me. I don't like that I'm so easily readable, but I like that she knows how to get me out of my own head, and, when necessary, let go. Not everyone will be accepting and I struggle to swallow that. Abby makes it easier.

By noon, my feet are sore and I'm starving and cranky. I've turned into one of Stephen King's horrish fictional creations. I text Abby and we meet at a pizza restaurant that gave me a very warm welcome. We walk in and a waitress directs us to a booth, but I asked for a table instead. Abby grins, and I feel like my skin is being pricked with needles. I bet she can read minds, or at least my mind, because she rolls her eyes at me and tells me I'm a wimp for being so uncomfortable with any emotion. I roll my eyes at her but stay silent. I stare at the menu and tell her to do the same. Twenty minutes later, we have a steaming pizza with mozzarella, tomatoes, basil, and herbs. She gets a Cherry Coke while I stick with Pepsi and a jug of iced water for us. I hate ice in water because it hurts me teeth, but Abby loves it.

When the waiter leaves, Abby gives me another one of her smiles. "You're being very generous today."

"Yeah, well. I want you to know I really appreciate you doing this."

"Well, I'm not completely doing this for you, you're welcome. I'm having fun. A lot of fun, actually."

"Me too," I say, smiling. Neither one of us were expecting to enjoy this project, but I'm glad we were wrong.
I sip my soda as Abby cuts the pizza into slices. We put slices into our plates and begin to eat once the rising steam withers. We eat, drink, talk, laugh, and come near tears. We think about our mother, who was equal parts loved as she was hurtful. It's nice to talk about how Mom wasn't perfect with someone who knew her as well as I did, maybe better. I never understood our parents, and maybe I never tried to. But Abby did. She tried to understand and love us all, even at our darkest, dirtiest lows. Even when loving us was hard, she never stopped. We're polar in this way, too. But I'm trying. And that's all anyone can hope for.

Chapter Fifty Eight

The fundraiser is short of one week away. I'm exhausted and the initial excitement has long worn off, and I struggle to stay conscious at work. My head's heavy and I'm nursing my third cup of black coffee by noon. I have almost no make-up, definitely not enough to cover the dark circles under my eyes. I don't eat when I'm stressed or tired, so my cheeks have hollowed, as several of my colleagues remind me. But I'm not doing this fundraiser for me, and if ten year olds can survive days without water or food in a t-shirt during a snowy winter, I better be able to handle a day of work in air conditioning with coffee, bagels, and at least two hours of sleep.

I close my eyes briefly and open them again as I brew another pot of coffee after emptying the last one. I hear footsteps but they don't register. They click obnoxiously loud against worn dirty tiles, and the sound irritates me.

"Mmh, I'm starving," Margie says. I turn to face her wordlessly and smile thinly.

Starving. What an exaggeration. She's not starving. She doesn't even know the meaning of the word. But I don't say this.

"Someone brought bagels. And cream cheese, I think. In the fridge."

She huffs. "Those are long stale. And they're out of French toast."

I roll my eyes at her, and as soon as I realize what I've done, I turn around and face my coffee cup on the counter.

"What's your problem?"

"Nothing. Sorry, I'm just tired."

"Oh. Long night?"

"Yeah. I was busy with this event thing I'm planning."

"Ooh, what kind of event?" she asks excitedly, anger forgotten. I envy that, but I also admire it. As much I judge this woman, no matter how crabby I get with her, she always forgives me instantly. As people should, because everyone has bad days. But I'm guilty of judgment without reason or kindness.

"A fundraiser for Syria," I say after a moment's hesitation. I don't know how she'll react. I already have enough racists in my life, and in my past, I was one of them.

"Nell, that's awesome. Good for you! Do you have a flyer or something with you? I'd love to come!"

I stare down at my coffee as the few bubbles dissipate, My mouth is open and I shut it once I realize it. I feel disgusted with myself and my tainted image of everyone. I believed so firmly in my judgment of people, and yet in the past couple months, I've realized that I've been wrong about everyone. Dad, Abby, and now Margie. Maybe myself as well. I'm not nearly as noble as I believed.

I turn to face Margie and smile. Her unnatural flame colored hair is in dire need of a haircut. She's average build and her looks are simple. The smoky eye and gaudy purple red lipstick is unfitting for her soft featured face. While heavy concealer and foundation hide the freckles on her face, I see her hands and legs are littered with them. She's in the customary white uniform, but she wears dangly earrings just barely professional, and a clanking bunch of silver bracelets. But she's much more than what she looks like she would be. I'm learning that everyone is more than their outermost layer.

"I have a couple extras in my bag. I'll remember to get you one." My voice is a hoarse whisper. She makes no mention of it.

We talk for a little longer before getting back to work. Well, she talks and I answer her many questions with awkward monosyllabic answers.

The rest of the day drags. I didn't pack a lunch and didn't have the time to buy one during my break, so despite my exhaustion, I decide to stop somewhere for lunch. As I'm grabbing my purse I hear my name from behind me. I turn and I am greeted with a friendly face.

Audrey Williams is as classy as her namesake. She has the darkest blue black hair I've witnessed, and it bounces in model worthy curls. Her skin is pale white but it is clear of any blemishes without makeup. She manages to look classy in a casual suit of black slacks that touch the skin just above her ankles, a matching blazer and a blue cotton blouse. She wears small black wedges and her nails are painted an adventurous blue, messily applied. Her teeth are perfect, which anyone can see because she's constantly smiling. Her eyebrows are full and natural. Despite her obvious beauty, I can't seem to envy her. She's too kind hearted and sweet. I admire her but I can't envy her.

"Hey, Nell! How are you? I feel like I haven't talked to you in forever."

I grin without realizing. "I'm good. I know, I miss you!" We talk for a while longer, before she asks me if I'm busy.

"No, I was just going to get something to eat. I didn't have lunch."

"Do you mind if I join you? I don't want to intrude or anything, but--"

"No, no! You should come. We can catch up."
She smiles. "Great. I'll grab something from my desk and meet you outside."

Chapter Fifty Nine

We end up meeting at a local Mexican restaurant. It's nothing fancy, and I've never been here before but Audrey makes it sound very tempting. I always thought she would make a great lawyer. I tell her this, but she only laughs good-naturedly

She recommends the beef tacos with their specialty sauce. But she gets that devious look on her face when she mentions the sauce, and I ask for a mild salsa instead. She playfully calls me boring, and she's kind of right. There's not much that's outstanding about me.

"Nice nails," I snicker, and tilt my head towards her finger painted blue. The nail polish has streaks in it and it misses parts of the nails and goes over onto the skin. I tell her it's refreshing to see a part of Audrey that's imperfect. She laughs, and this time, I feel like it's at me, and it's the kind of laugh that makes me get defensive.

"Messy? I'm always messy. But these babies were

actually courtesy of my niece and nephew. Andrew and Andrea. They wanted to paint something."

"That's adorable. And further proving my point. Maybe you're messy, but in that nonchalant, cool as a cucumber kind of way."

"Cool? Nonchalant? Honey, you haven't seen me on my monthly breakdown."

"I guess. It's just… you pull off everything so well. Even when you're completely uncertain, you're so… confident and bold. You're honest to everyone, including yourself. I wish I had that."

"Are you kidding? I might be confident but you have this drive I've never seen in anyone else. I mean-" she chuckles, "I remember when I told you Paul tweeted that crap about me. You hunted that scumbag down and made him take it down and apologize. I bet he cried himself to sleep that night just thinking about you."

I roll my eyes. "Whatever."

"I'm serious. Or this fundraiser project you started? Who just comes up with that? You're stubborn as hell, but it also means you're just as driven. When you want something, you get it."

"Yeah. And when I inevitably reach a time where I don't get what I want, it breaks me down until there is almost no possibility of return. I get so… attached."

She smiles softly, like she knows something. "Can't argue with that. And yeah-" she's whispering now, "maybe it gets you in deep trouble sometimes. But it also get you to crazy places that other people don't even bother dreaming of because they don't believe like you do. And I've never seen anyone care so fiercely about the people in your circle like you do. No one."

We stay silent until the food comes, and we sip our drinks in the meantime. Our taco platter comes on a rustic black pan with high sides. It has wooden handles met with a metal rim. The waiter sets down a tray of sauces and tells us what each one is.

Heavy steam rises from the tacos. I reach for one and then get the mild sauce.

"Oh, try the special sauce! Don't you trust me?" Audrey says with a scary Cheshire cat grin.

"With my bank account and future children? Absolutely. With my food? Absolutely not."

She snorts. "Nice to know you've got your priorities straight."

"Don't I know it."

She laughs and I join in. As we cover our tacos with sauce and sour cream, Audrey looks up at me. "You seem different. Happier. There's this… glow."

I laugh nervously. "Inside? Are you sure? Because I've been using this new exfoliating cleanser."

She shakes her head. "Your skin sucks. There are freaking bags under your eyes. Big ugly purple ones. And you look pale as a ghost."

Now I snort. "You're calling me pale?"

"Seriously, though. You look like a steaming pile of

crap."

"I appreciate it."

"Are you just not sleeping? What's the deal?"

"I sleep, just not as much as before. With this fundraiser a week away, I've been busy."

My aloof explanation doesn't remove the worried expression like I expected. In fact, it only seems to worsen. "You still need to take care of yourself."

"Eh, it's only a part time thing. I'll be back to normal on Monday. Don't worry."

She stays silent.

"Oh my God, you're right! These tacos are amazing. Hot though. I think I burnt my tongue. Why are you still staring?   Am I that pretty?"

"I know you're… excited about your event. But Nell, it won't just be this event. Monday will come and you'll have something else on your plate. And then you'll be saying all will be normal by the week after that. And then after that."

"It's just a one time gig-"

"No. No, it won't be. I'd bet my car on it."

"And why is that such a bad thing?" I wipe my mouth with the napkin and put down the taco.

"It's not bad at all, as long as you stay balanced. As long as you stay healthy and functioning."

"Kids are dying out there, and I'm not just going to-"

"You're fundraiser isn't going to stop those kids from dying."

We're silent for a moment. "What's your problem?" I

ask.

"I'm not trying to offend you. It's just that, while I think you're doing a great thing with this fundraiser, you're losing perspective. What's happening out there is awful and your fundraiser will make a difference. But Nell, you can't get so absorbed in this. Life's unfair. You're here and those kids aren't. And no amount of stress or self-guilt is going to change that. I just… I don't want to see you broken. You have an unbelievably huge heart. Make it your strength, not your fall."

My mouth opens after a minute, but I shut it and listen back to her words. I swallow my immediate defensive reaction and allow myself to be offended, but not so much to the point of no reason. Once the shocking anger wears off to a subtle shimmer, I realize she's not completely wrong. Doesn't mean I like it. Who likes to be wrong?

In the end, I just say, "Okay." Not my most eloquent moment, but I'm just proud I didn't lose it. Hers or mine, I'm not sure.

I guess I'm not as awesome at hiding my emotions as I thought, because Audrey touches my arm and smiles.

"Let it go, Nell. It's okay. Why don't we just finish our food and then we can go out for ice cream or something."

"I can never say no to ice cream." I smile and let it go.

Well, the second part is questionable.

"Actually, pass me your special sauce."

She gives me an amused look. "You sure you can handle the heat?"

"No, but I need to do something crazy and stupid. I

just- just pass me the sauce."

"Well, if you insist." She smirks.

I snatch the white miniature bowl and forgoing the spoon, I messily pour a stream of the sauce next to my tacos. I set the sticky bowl down and lick a finger. My eyes water, my nose burns, and I stick my tongue out like a sweaty dog.

"Ah, hot, hot, hot!"

Audrey laughs, snorting. "Really? I had no idea."

"Shut up and pass me the water."

"Do you regret needing to do something crazy and stupid?"

I grin. "Not one bit."

Chapter Sixty

"I think I literally burnt my tongue."

Audrey laughs. "I bet you do. You're full of surprises, Whitaker."

I try not to smile at that. I like being called unpredictable. I can tell Audrey knows this, as she takes one look at me and snorts, shaking her head.

I lick my triple chocolate fudge brownie ice cream cone and Audrey takes a spoonful of her low fat raspberry sorbet. I roll my eyes. Low fat sorbet. Apparently nothing gets past this woman because she gives me this accusing look and says,

"You're so judgmental."

"Keeps me perky."

She snorts again. "You? Perky? Yeah, and Donald Trump is a babe."

"Ew! Don't ever say that again!"

"It's an apt comparison. But you're right, that does sound pretty disgusting."

"You sure that's not because you're eating a low fat sorbet made of coconut milk? That is like when Mom would tell me she bought pizza and I got all excited. Until I realized pizza meant crunchy wheat crust with feta, mushrooms, and this curdled looking vinaigrette. Ugh."

Audrey's silent for a moment and when I turn to face her, she's doing that weird stare again.

"What?"

"You just... I don't think you've ever mentioned your mom like that since..."

"She died? It's okay, you can say it."

"I-I'm sorry. I didn't mean-"

"No, don't be."

"No worries," she says quietly, but heavily.

"Do you miss her?" she asks after a long moment.

I let out a heavy breath. "Yeah. Yeah, I do. But not in that crushing, wormhole kind of way. There's this heaviness, and I don't think it'll ever go away. But for the first time since she died, I feel like I can breathe. It's a good feeling."

Audrey smiles the kind of smile that makes you wonder if she's a seventy year old woman stuck in the body of a twenty something. I smile back nervously. But I mean it.

We talk until night greets us, and once the energy from

the euphoria is depleted, we decide to go home. But I give Audrey the fundraiser's flyer before she leaves, and tell her to make sure she comes. I don't need her there, but it would be touching if she came.

Then I go home. I go home and moments before sleep takes me, I see my mother's beautiful face. No one ever believed her to be stunning, but I couldn't disagree more. They said her cheekbones were too sharp, cheeks too hollow, eye too icy in their depths of blue. She was too much of everything, everything I wished I had. I think about her face and her rare, beautiful smile that I used to measure my success on. I think about her perfect teeth that would never be on display. I think of her short red hair I would twirl my fingers around as a child. I see her too small, too angular ears. I see her hands that would rub my head when I couldn't fall asleep.

I see my mother and I fall in love with the world just a little more. I see my mother and I regain some of my faith.

Chapter Sixty One

Every time I stand here, at the footsteps of my father's home, I feel imminent doom. I stand here, and I feel like I'm twelve again, completely unsure of myself and everything that was once so clear. But today is different. I am still scared of what will happen, and I still feel my fears overload my brain. But I'm still in control. And I'm not twelve anymore.

I expect my courage to fade once I see my father, in his

expected plaid and jeans combo. When it persists, I expect my courage to fade when he turns his back to me and leaves for the kitchen as I shut the door he opens. For the last time, I hope.

The courage persists, even when a little room is made for unstoppable fear. I slide off my sandals and walk to the kitchen. But before I do, I stand in the foyer under our chandelier, his chandelier. The one my mother chose. I wear my favorite blue jeans and sweatshirt from college. I look like me. I used to think that was my weakness, and I almost changed. But I don't need professional strength today. I need to be my father's daughter. I need what I believe is my best strength and sometimes my most dire downfall: ever persisting determination for the people I love.

With this, I walk into the kitchen. I see the door to his office is open, and I can smell the stench of oil paints and his chemicals that I've come to know as the smell of my father's creativity. His niche. Something I thought I never had.

He's sitting at a counter, staring at the cover of this book.

"Fountainhead. Nice choice," I say in an attempt to begin a conversation.

He shrugs. "Not like I plan on reading it. Thing's so big I could probably murder someone with it."

I laugh at his serious expression, so unfitting with his sarcastic line.

After my awkward burst of laughter, the room becomes silent again, save for the scraping of chair against hardwood as

I pull up next to Dad. He cringes at the noise.

"What do you want, Nell? Because if you're here to yell at me… Well. I'm not in the mood. Maybe another time." He sounds bitter but I can't blame him.

"No. No yelling," I'm whispering now, but I know he can hear me.

"I just want to listen. I want to listen to you. I keep thinking I need to talk to you and you're the one that needs to listen. But I was wrong. I'm so busy being angry and tired from misplaced anger, I never considered just shutting up, you know? And I know I'm starting to sound like a broken record here, but I'm sorry, Dad. I'm sorry."

I fidget with the hem of my sleeve as silence suffocates me. Finally, he speaks. "What did you want to talk about?"

"Anything you want. I just want to know my dad again." He turns to me and gives me this very sad serious smile that looks so wrong on him. He stares at me as if he's looking at someone else. Like he's remembering all over again, the things he so desperately wishes to forget. He used to tell me right when mom died that I reminded him of her. It never made any sense to me, because Abby looks like her identical twin. I look nothing like my mother, and I didn't think I acted anything like her, either. But now, I'm starting to see what Dad saw. I'm starting to understand, because I've finally decided to try.

And then his smile becomes kind and warm. "Why don't we move to the couch, after I make some coffee? This could take a while, if that's alright with you. I'd like to get to know you too, kiddo."

I smile gently. "I can make the coffee?"

He looks at me all vulnerable and struggles to smile. "Okay."

Once our mugs are filled to the brim, we talk. We talk for hours about everything under the sun. We talk and I feel like I've gotten a missed treasure back. And when all is said, I ask if he'll come to the fundraiser. He says he'll think about it.

That's all I can ask for.

And when the night ends, my scattered puzzle pieces align a little more. And I begin to become whole again.

Chapter Sixty Two

My heels wobble in the grass. I knew I should've worn my comfy shoes, but Abby insisted I dress up. I regret listening to her about much of my outfit. The makeup feels heavy, and every few minutes, I get the urge to rub at my eyes to get rid of some of the powdery stuff. But I resist the urge, because the raccoon eyes look wouldn't fare well. I am caked in foundation and concealer, blush, contour, eyeliner that I redid at least four times and only partially succeeding the last, shimmery eyeshadow, and one too many layers of mascara. And then there's the lipstick. It's this matte, dark purple red color that is simultaneously stunning and scary. I think the blush was a mistake, considering I'm sure my flushed face more than makes up for my usual lack of color.

The only thing I don't regret accepting from Abby is the dress. I'd completely forgotten to buy something for the event, or maybe I just figured I'd wear something old. I was never the type to buy new dresses just for an occasion, but Abby always has been. And I grudgingly admit she has impeccable taste. It's a beautiful black dress with matching pantyhose and a cream colored blazer. The neck of the dress is embroidered in elegant bluish stones. It's simple and modest so I don't feel mortified in it, but it's also classy and elegant.

But right now, I can't think much about what I'm wearing. The fundraiser is set to start in twenty minutes, and there are already way too many people here. Abby kept telling me to plan for more people, but I refused. In the end she caved, and I thought I'd won. It's clear now that I was wrong. People are still coming, and already there are too many people for the refreshments I have, or for the speakers I rented. This is going to be a disaster.

I run to Abby and squeeze her shoulders. She winces. "Abby! God, you were right! Do you see how many people are here? We don't have enough chairs, or drinks, or food, or speakers. And, oh my God! This is going to be a total flop. God, why didn't I just listen to you? You were right, I'm stubborn. I'm sorry, I'm so sorry. Please, just fix this." I'm breathless when I'm done.

But she just smirks. "While I appreciate the apology, what do you expect me to do? Just find us a genie and ask for five more fills of punch? Even I can't work Aladdin's kind of magic, hon."

I stare at her in horror and open my mouth to rant. Thank God she stops me. Who knows what I would've let out in a stream?

"But, I don't need a genie, because I am the glorious Abigail Whitaker."

And then she bows, and I can't even roll my eyes because I'm trying not to puke, despite my very empty stomach, save for coffee and pretzels with peanut butter.

"I rented extra chairs and speakers. I also brought plenty of refills. Although even I wasn't expecting this crowd. But it'll be fine. There is definitely no shortage of food, but for the chairs, some people can stand. And I'm sure some people brought mats and chairs, since it's a park."

I grin so wide I think my face muscles actually crack. They've never worked this hard before. "God, I love you." And then I squeeze her lungs with my arms and my smile only fades a little.

"Okay, okay. It's gonna be a okay." I let out a breath.

"Aren't you happy I don't listen to you?" Abby says with this very cheeky smile. I can't even be mad about it, because I'm too busy reeling.

"Yeah, yeah."

Abby chuckles. "I'll go tell the guys to bring the chairs and extra speakers."

I'm barely listening at this point. Instead, I look around me and smile. The whole event is under four huge white tents put together. Colorful streamers decorate the edges. Innumerable lines of white cloth chairs face a wooden stage that looks bigger than I imagine it to be. One of the tech guys, Michael, is fiddling with the slide show and I see as it turns on and a slide show of pictures appear. Pictures of Syria and their people, of all the organizations we will donate to. There are these pictures of trucks filled with food, water, shoes, and clothes, all being passed to desperate refugees. But my favorite picture of all is one of the kids. There's this group of young boys playing in the snow and throwing chunks of it at each other. They're laughing and smiling, most of them. They have dirt smeared on their faces, and you can see the shabby tents in the background, where the solemn women and other children are. Some look at the camera with an empty expression, others look directly at me with a carefree look of love. As if the camera just happened to catch them in a moment of laughter. The boys are so handsome with their vibrant colored eyes, long lashes, and even in their unfitting mismatched clothes and shoes. They don't look unknowing. They know, more than me and everyone else here. They know about the horrors of life, the tragedies, the hopelessness. They know feelings that I will never have to understand, nor do I want to. They know all this and yet they're laughing as if someone's just told the funniest joke in the world. And they're in the midst of a snowball fight, as if they allow themselves to be children despite all the events that want to force them to be otherwise solemn creatures that have lost all hope. No. These boys have hope. And I'm going to give them good reason to.

Abby calls my name because there's an issue with the main speakers and one of the wires are broken. Chaos at its finest. It's crazy for the next twenty minutes, and it only gets crazier. Despite the open plains of the park, these people chose to come here and be crammed in a tent, just to help these people. Or maybe it's just for the punch. I love them all the same. We start ten minutes late, right as my phone buzzes from a text. It's from Dad: I'm here. I see you.

I smile and feel like my heart has just been physically touched. I feel I'll become reacquainted with the feeling quite well in the next two hours. I text him back with a thank you and a smile. I silence my phone and look for him in the crowd, but I don't see him. I don't think it matters though. He's here and that means everything to me.

"... And now let us welcome Penelope Whitaker to the stage, the very reason for this event."

The crowd applauses and it only embellishes the burning anxiety. It's not just in my chest as my heart beats a million times a minute, but in my entire body. My being. My sweaty hands flutter, and my toes try to curl. My legs shake and I feel my clothes stick to me. I've thought about this moment so many times in such clear ringing detail, and I always thought my mind would be racing faster than my heart but it isn't. My mind is completely silent. I can't even hear my thoughts, or create coherent sentences in my brain. I just feel, and it is terrifying.

I walk up the stage as I practiced an hour before, and Abby hands me the microphone. I look at her in panic, and she just smiles at me. The grin she wore a second ago is replaced with a smile of comfort and encouragement. It helps, surprisingly. I don't let myself finish the thoughts of panic about my Dad or the eyes watching me. At least six hundred and thirty six pairs of eyes. I take a deep breath as the crowd settles. Then I focus on Ameer, because he is the true reason for this event.

"Thank you for coming here tonight. I appreciate each and every one you for showing up. I want to give my sister, Abby, a special thank you. I couldn't have done it without her. I also want to thank all the volunteers for their contribution. You've all given a part of yourselves to this event, and I appreciate you guys. Thank you.

"But there is one person I would like to thank that could not attend today. His name was Ameer. Just Ameer. He never told me his last name. In fact, he didn't tell me much of anything about him. But there are four things I learned about him. One, he couldn't have been older than 12. Two, he loved flying kites, even though he had no talent for it. Three, he was completely and truly alone. No family or friends with him. And four, he died because no one cared to help him."

The crowd feels quieter now, despite the crying baby and children's hushed conversations. My anxiety takes a backseat in my brain, and all I can think about is Ameer.

"A few months ago, I decided to go to Syria to help in a refugee camp. But long story short, I got stuck in Istanbul for a few days. That's a city in Turkey, and also one of the most beautiful places I have ever had the pleasure of seeing. It is also one of the most heartbreaking and awakening places I've ever been. There are these Syrian children everywhere. And not only children. Women, men, couples. The streets are littered with them. But I most distinctly remember the children.

One night on my way back from this restaurant, I saw this boy. Curled up against this disgusting dirty brick wall of some building. It was pouring outside and I was just thinking about how I was going to have to do laundry the next day because my jeans were soaked. I was thinking about how unlucky it was that I'd only worn my thin green jacket that day. I was so frustrated I almost didn't notice him. But there he was. His knees were pressed against his chest, and he only wore thin frayed jeans and a baggy t-shirt that was covered in blood and dirt. And he was so skinny. I saw frail bones and pale skin. No flesh on him. Even his cheeks were gone, as if his face went inward. His hair was tangled, mangy, oily, and I later discovered it had an awful deal of lice in it. And he wore men's flip flops. His feet were so dirty that his nails were black. And just like that, I forgot my anger.

The worst was that expression he wore. Completely blank, like he didn't even realize the rain that soaked him. No shivering or tears or mumbling. Just pure blankness. Except not really, because I could almost see the memories that circled through his head, like a nightmare that was set on replay. I never found out what those night mares were. He talked only twice. Once to tell me his name. And the other to tell me not to help him when I discovered the lice. I didn't listen.

Slowly, I would discover him. How he loved flying kites, but he was awful at it. Or how he never really reached out to the other children. And the fact that I wasn't the only one drawn to him. Everyone connected with him. And he was so handsome. Despite his awful state, he had the most beautiful green eyes and the thickest lashes. His skin was paper white, and he had this perfectly shaped small nose and pink cheeks.

The more I found out about him, the more I loved him. And I swore to myself that I would never make that mistake again. I would never abandon anyone like that, especially a child. So this is what this fundraiser's about. It's about not leaving anyone behind, because then that makes us responsible when these children are lost. But before we do that, I'd like to take a moment to remember Ameer. Please join me. I will never forget his face or his kindness. I will never forget what the world lost the day he died. And I hope none of you do, either. The boy deserves to be remembered, because he possessed the beautiful power of strength. Even as a little boy alone in a new city, this boy fought on."

And then I breathe and say, "So join me in a moment of silence."

The park becomes wrapped in relative silence. There is still the sound of kids screeching in excitement, dogs barking, the laughter and chatter. I heard the heavy sound of hundreds breathing. I hear the occasional whines of a toddler. And I hear the wind that flows into the barrier of the tents and makes flapping noises in my mind. But I only listen for Ameer.

I close my eyes and clasp my clammy hands. I see the smile of a beautiful boy, covered in filth and yet so innocent. I see him curled up against that wall, but I focus on the memory of him fiddling with the kite. Eyes closed, hands twitching, and smiling just barely. So free. I see him, and I feel my heart hurt. And I feel tears leak from my eyes at the thought of him. I cry as I say goodbye. I wish him well, wherever he is. And I tell him I love him. Even if he can't hear me, I need to say it. And then my eyes open. I breathe in the sweaty damp air and I feel my chest lighten from its months of heaving. And as I finish wishing goodbye to my past of Ameer, I greet the present and the future.

Whatever it may hold.

"Fiction is the truth inside the lie." -Stephen King